# Devilry In The Delta:
## A Mississippi Mojo Thriller

Mary S. Palmer

&

Paula Lenor Webb

Mary S. Palmer & Paula Lenor Webb

An Intellect Publishing Book
Copyright 2022 Mary S. Palmer & Paula Lenor Webb

ISBN: 978-1-954693-56-2

Front cover design by Abe Partridge

First Edition:  2022

FV -5



Cover art by singer and artist Abe Partridge

Visit the website: www.MississippiMurderBook.com

Intellect Publishing, LLC
6581 County Road 32, Suite 1195
Point Clear, AL 36564
www.IntellectPublishing.com

# Dedication

To my sister, Jean Montiel, who read stories I wrote at age twelve—and told me to finish them.

Mary S. Palmer


To William C. Webb, aka Dear Old Dad, my best friend.

Paula Lenore Webb

Mary S. Palmer & Paula Lenor Webb

# Acknowledgements

To all of our readers for their diligence in finding things that needed changing and other suggestions that made this book capture the attention of readers. They are David Preston, Mike Turner, Mary Duffy, Muriel Nero, and Michael Campbell.

Mary S. Palmer & Paula Lenor Webb

# Prologue

The endless rainy days in the Mississippi Delta finally stopped. Water that previously flowed across the roads remained in the ditches, some water in potholes dried up, and the mud still there split and cracked. Hunter Harley leaned his body as muscular as a pit bull's against his patrol car parked at the edge of the Sunflower River. From the corner of his eye, he spotted a fire ant navigating the muddy cracks surrounding his boot. He sympathized with the small creature, relating to its struggle to explore new terrain. Hunter had to do the same when he moved to Cleveland; in many situations, he was still finding his way.

What happened a few months ago shouldn't have, but it did. Hunter leaned on the warm hood of his car and watched the sun set into the horizon of an orange sky. The Sunflower River flowing at a trickle made him wonder if Mamma Cheche's body would someday rise up out of its banks.

Today things were peaceful, but not so long ago this remote area had been a hub of activity. Hunter used all resources available to search the water and surrounding fields for her body, but nothing was found. Many locals, especially those familiar with Cheche's mojo, felt it was entirely too much unusual activity for a place like Cleveland, Mississippi. They prayed for things to return to being nice and calm with any unnerving activities kept under wraps and solved without all the hullabaloo.

Uncontrollable thoughts raced through the sheriff's mind and dark memories crept in on his reflective moment by the body of water. A bead of sweat from under his Stetson hat ran down his cheek as he recalled the time in Dallas when he stared out at Lake Ray with a gun in his right hand. Moonlight shining off the polished gun barrel, he had been ready to use it to solve his problems. Then, sanity overruled despair, a hint of faith eased into his heart. He remembered a preacher once told him God and time could fix anything. Giving in to those thoughts, Hunter vowed to find a way to rectify his mistakes and move on.

So, Hunter started over, he expected to be the sheriff of this quiet, small town for a short time, but he experienced the opposite. He still saw remnants of police tape among the weeds, marking where a couple of months into his term as interim sheriff, skeletal remains of a famous blues singer, Goldie Parsons, floated to the surface during a flood. It had ended years of speculation and lore, and the action began.

Hunter kicked at a jagged bit of dried clay in front of his boot blocking the path of a determined fire ant. Things that happened in Dallas were not fixed; but he was feeling better and the events of his life in Cleveland had helped him come to terms with the mistakes he made in Texas. *I came here to escape Dallas and my failure there. Ha! What I expected to be an easy job turned into investigating one of the largest cold cases ever. Nobody realized Goldie Parsons was murdered until over half a century after he went missing. Now that's a cold case, a very cold case. Yet, I got the job done.*

Hunter's heart ached when the memories returned in a flash, still as fresh in his mind as if they'd just happened. He was astounded at how Goldie Parsons became famous after cutting only one record in Memphis. He then thought about the Tollar family, the love and loss they experienced, and who tempted fate by hiring a killer. So much drama had happened since that moment. Hunter's eye twitched as he took off his cowboy hat, ran his hand through his dark hair, damp with sweat, and put it back on. It wasn't like any case he would have expected, things weren't resolved like he hoped, but at least he'd solved the case.

Hunter was no longer Cleveland, Mississippi's newest resident; the population increased last month when Goldie's granddaughter, Shannon, moved into the old Tollar Plantation house with two children in tow. She had called him before leaving Washington, D. C. to talk about the destination of Goldie's remains.

"Hunter," Shannon told him, "I want my family to be together. I am talking to the Sunflower County Board of Supervisors to create a family cemetery on the Tollar Plantation. I plan to have Goldie's, my grandmother, and mother's remains moved there. If you don't mind, keep Goldie's bones at the city morgue till the rest come from Mobile. Once I move down there and get the kids settled, we will have a proper ceremony. I don't want to make a big deal out of this, but I do want to show Goldie the respect he never got when he was alive."

Then she laughed, "As if my life wasn't colorful enough, I am the guardian of two kids! My half brother and sister. Our dad died and his second wife, a trophy wife, didn't want them. All Frederica cares about is Frederica. Her name suits her; she was born during Hurricane Frederic. She's past thirty now, but she's flitting, or storming, around like a teenager. I'll fill you in on the rest over a cup of coffee when I get into town and move into the family property."

Hunter shook his head in wonder, the last time he saw Shannon she was a sharp-witted Washington D. C. lawyer in a tight suit…and single. *I bet that story is going to be an interesting one. Timing is everything.* Harley was strangely attracted to Shannon Brown; he had realized how much her flaming red hair suited her personality the moment he met her. She gave up her prestigious city life as a high-powered attorney and moved to Cleveland. *From fancy lattes to fields of cotton. I wonder what kind of culture shock she's going to feel. Maybe more than I did.*

Hunter walked to the river's edge, dirt crunching under his boots, took in a deep breath, and closed his eyes. A flashback of Goldie's skull resting in the mud crossed his mind and he opened his eyes wide to shake the image. *No mojo for me. No vision. I'm remembering what I saw. Damn, it wasn't the first time I'd seen remains of a human body but seeing them here was unexpected. Kind of caught me off guard. Ah, it reminds me of Mama Cheche. Smart woman. Knew when her time was up and took care of it in her own, inimitable way.* He shook his head. His heart hurt a little as he stared at the sun disappearing in the distance. *Maybe she did have the power of the mojo. If there is such a magical charm, I heard a few rumors that Goldie had it but ignored it. It would be odd if it wound up with his granddaughter.*

Stooping, Hunter picked up a wad of packed dirt and tossed it into what was left of the river during the dry spell. It barely caused a ripple. *Why am I even thinking about the mojo? I can't hide in this town forever. Richard Grimes is graduating and is going to come home soon. He'll take over as sheriff like his father before him. I will need to move on. Where do I go?* Whether his deputy, Zita Rocconi, played a part in that decision, he was still unable to admit it. He remembered the sweetness of her favorite perfume and breathed deeply. Forcing such thoughts from his mind, Hunter turned and walked back to his car. *Another day; another dollar.*

# Devilry In The Delta:
## A Mississippi Mojo Thriller

# Chapter 1

On his way into town from the Shackum Up Inn, Hunter watched the sunrise through a cotton field, and droplets of dew shone on the puffy white pods like diamonds. Next, the cathead biscuits at Levenia's diner were spectacular; slathered with butter and homemade jam, they melted in his mouth. Then, Zita's smiling face greeted him when he walked into his office. Sniffing, he savored the aroma of hazelnut coffee brewing in the percolator. Zita must have turned on the pot when she saw him pull into his parking spot.

Zita strolled into Hunter's office iPad in her right hand and ready to go over their itinerary for the week. She liked using the tablet to take notes, but Hunter preferred pencil and paper. When he was offered one for work, he politely refused.

Hunter poured himself a cup of coffee and breathed in the aroma. He flashed Zita a smile as he sat in his chair behind his desk and leaned back.

"You look perky today, Hunter. Did your day start out right?"

Hunter nodded. "It did. For once, it seems like everything fits into its proper place. How about you?" The ring of his desk phone interrupted the conversation.

As the phone rang, the name *Richard Grimes* and the area code, New York, flashed across the digital screen. He pressed the speaker button and said, "Hello, Rich…" before Richard blurted out, "I don't know if this is good news or bad for you, but I've decided not to return to Cleveland. I've had a taste of a different world, and I like it. I'm going to law school and become an attorney."

Aware of how this would affect him, Hunter's grip on the armrest of his chair tightened. He saw Zita's eyes widen when he replied, "Your family's not going to like that, Rich."

"Nope, they don't. Mamma cried when I told her. I've already caught Hell for not conforming to family tradition, but I have to follow my heart. You can't do a good job anyhow if you don't like what you're doing."

Hunter watched Zita go slack in her chair, almost dropping her iPad. Richard cleared his throat over the phone. "Speaking of that, they might not want me back anyway. You're doing a great job. If you decide to stay in Cleveland as sheriff, without me in the race, I doubt that you'll have any competition."

A pregnant pause followed, and Hunter gasped. He willed himself not to slam the phone against the wall. He wasn't ready for this. He was at a loss because he didn't know the answer. He stammered, trying not to let the anger creep into his voice. "Well, Richard, I, er, I don't know. This comes as a surprise. You know, the Goldie Parsons case got a lot--I mean a lot--of publicity. I've had offers for jobs from Atlanta, Mobile, and New Orleans. On the other hand, Cleveland didn't turn out to be the peaceful burg I expected."

"Ah, yeah, but Hunter, you had its biggest case ever fall into your lap. What a fluke! Maybe you were meant to be there to solve it, the only one who had the skills to do so. Nothing like human remains washing up on the riverbank ever happened before, so it's unlikely that it will again. Hells bells! Issuing parking tickets, and containing domestic disturbances are usually Cleveland's biggest deals. Going to the liquor store and watching people bang on the door after closing time is our citizens' most exciting entertainment. Things have calmed down. You should stay and enjoy it."

Hunter took Richard's advice and remained in Cleveland. Given the circumstances and the nagging curiosity at the back of his mind about Zita and Shannon, he ran for sheriff and the elections came and went with no competition. It was as if he'd simply moved from one season of life into the next.

*     *     *

"Hunter, a change is in order. You know what you have to do, right?" Zita told him when he walked into the office the day after the votes were tallied from November 6th and he had an easy win since he was the only one running for the sheriff's position. "You can't stay at the Shackum Up Inn," she said. "Now that you'll be here a while, you need place of your own in town."

"Zita," Hunter grimaced. "I do not want to house hunt, I hate it and moving."

"No worries!" she smiled. "I will find the perfect place for you!"

A part of Hunter felt like this might be a bad idea, but his stomach churned at the thought of dealing with real estate agents and financing. "Okay," he agreed, "let's see what you can do." Zita's grin made him cringe.

In a matter of weeks, Zita found him a second-floor loft of a converted grocery store only two blocks from the office.

"Hunter, you will love it!" she bragged. Her eyes lit up like a campfire on a dark night. "These loft apartments downtown are so interesting and I found a perfect one for you. The owner occupies the downstairs as his home and workshop, and he converted the second floor into a nice apartment. The rent is reasonable, too. The owner is out of town right now, but I have the key." She held it up. "He told me to go ahead and show it to you. He is a huge blues' fan; better yet, he's enthralled with us and the whole Goldie Parsons thing." She tugged on his sleeve. "Come on, I can't wait for you to see it. Let's walk over there."

Zita led the way out the office door. It creaked as Hunter pulled it closed behind him.  He took a momentary glance towards his patrol car parked on the street.

"Zita, wait. What is that stuff all over my car?"

Zita didn't see it at first. "What stuff? Oh, it's just dust… wait. No way! It can't be."

Hunter was confused, "Can't be what?"

He walked over to see large puffs of dust on the doors of his typically spotless patrol car. "It looks like it was put there intentionally, but what is it?" He started to run his finger through it.

"Stop, Hunter, don't touch it. Best to take your car down to the carwash when we are done and get it cleaned again. You made someone mad, I think. It might be Voodoo powder."

"You have to be kidding! Voodoo powder?"

"Oh yes, the story goes that if you touch it, you will go crazy and die. Notice how much is on the door handles? No telling what it is made of. Could also be a prank, but best not to take chances." Her brow turned into furrows.

Hunter sighed. "Things are already crazy enough. Okay, let's go look at the place. Nothing is damaged here; we need a walk, I think."

Zita was right, the apartment was an easy walk from the office. It was cool under the magnificent oak trees lining the sidewalk that led to the converted grocery store, one of many once owned by Chinese immigrants in the Delta. The owner kept the front of the building looking like it did sixty years ago when it was Joe Wang's Market. Even the original phone booth by the former front door of the business still stood in its place. Hunter checked and he heard a dial tone when he picked up the receiver.

He approached the wide, gray steps that ran along the side of the building to the second-floor apartment. Just outside the door a small porch had a roof to keep off the rain. *It also provides a good way to see what is going on outside the door without being obvious,* thought Hunter.

Zita picked up pace, bounding up the stairs, wood creaking on every step. He watched her in admiration, grateful to have someone to help him take care of these sorts of things. He was a few steps behind her when something moving caught the corner of his eye. The black animal scurried off before he could identify it.

"Hunter! This place is great!" Zita called from inside the apartment, holding the door open for him to enter. His attention was drawn back to the excitement in Zita's eyes. She had the prettiest eyes.

She was right. When Hunter entered the solid wooden door engraved with various birds, he felt comfortable in the large, open living room. It would be suitable for entertaining. *That is an impressive design on the door! It's very artistic.*

Hunter was ready to invite friends over to his home again. It was time for the next step in recovering from the hard times he experienced in Texas. He couldn't entertain at the Shackum Up Inn since it was just a one room row house. He'd have space, plus, he'd become accepted as more of a permanent resident now. Since the Goldie Parson's case, people greeted him in the street with a handshake, nod of the head, or a wave from their cars. The positive attention was both strange and pleasant.

"Hunter, this place is huge!" Zita remarked as she strolled around. The front door opened into the living room to the right and a large, industrial kitchen to the left.

"Zita," he called out, "isn't that an Erik cooking range with double ovens? That's an extra-wide Erik fridge, too. Like the ones they make in Greenwood, Mississippi." Hunter pulled open one of the large ovens to see a setup for a rotisserie rack inside. His thoughts turned to the pulled pork and BBQ sauce he could make and how evenly his homemade Texas cheese bread would come out in the second oven. He looked around to see the Erik emblem on the over-the-range microwave and the dishwasher. It was a dream kitchen.

Hunter's eyes then followed the large beams that hovered over the kitchen and the vaulted ceiling covering the entire space. The twelve feet tall walls caused his footsteps to echo as he walked around the area in his solid heeled boots. The main corridor of the room led to two large bedrooms beyond the kitchen and living room: one on the left and one on the right. The room on the left had a plain bathroom, all white tile, even the countertops, but it had two doors. One door opened to the living room and kitchen and the other door offered access from the bedroom. The larger bedroom on the right had a smaller, private bathroom. *Perfect for me,* thought Hunter.

Beyond the bedrooms were two wide double doors, obviously leftover from the grocery store days. With arms like whips, Hunter pushed one open to see the spacious warehouse beyond. Motion detector lights automatically flickered on, flooding the space with light. Hunter saw huge canvases of all shapes and sizes and odd bits of material from tractors and cars. He wondered how such large pieces made it into the space until he spotted the old elevator lift located in the back corner and another set of large double doors leading to a backstairs exit.

"Zita, what exactly does the owner of this building do for a living?" Hunter asked.

"Oh, you will love him. He is an internationally known artist, Victor Von Horst, but we all call him 'V.' It's his trademark. This must be where he stores his materials for his creations. Fascinating!" She cocked her head. "Well, what do you think?"

A gourmet cook, starving to create again, Hunter thought of the Erik stove and didn't hesitate. "Yes," he nodded. "I like it. I will take it."

"Yea!" Embracing her boss, she kissed him on the cheek. Hunter couldn't deny he liked the warmth of her lips. He turned his head to hide the smile she brought to his face.

Within a week, Hunter received the lease agreement from V's Memphis lawyer, who noted V was installing one of his pieces in New York, signed the necessary papers and mailed them back.

When he moved out of his room at the Shackum Up Inn, he didn't have many possessions. He filled the back seat of the police car with his clothes, shoved his laptop amongst them to keep it safe. Next to it he put a bundle of folders full of notes about his last case in Dallas. He also packed the trunk carefully with his collection of boots. The hat boxes, containing his Stetson, Justin, and Resistol hats, were laid in the front passenger seat.

On a second trip, he loaded his car with treasured family items he brought from Texas: his parents' wedding china, a set of everyday dishes, and a box of drinking glasses decorated with large gold stars, all were taken from his mother's house when she passed. He included several place settings of sterling silver given to him by his mother; one set she'd received as a wedding gift, and the other she'd bought for Hunter when he found the right woman to marry. They'd never been removed from the flannel wrapping.

As he closed the passenger door of the car, he took one last look at his home for the past year, the Pink Palace, a converted rickety old one room shack. He was moving up in this small town in Cleveland, Mississippi. He stopped by the Delta Diner to say goodbye to Levenia. "Now that I have a kitchen," he said, "I'll probably be cooking my own breakfast a lot of the time, but I promise to continue to be a customer. See you soon."

Levenia assured him it was no problem saying, "I'm happy for you. You're welcome back anytime."

Hunter made the short trip back to his new apartment and was surprised by a large box that rested at the bottom of the steps. *It's here!*

As a Texan wanting to stay with western decor, as soon as he signed the lease, he bought a deer head by the famous taxidermist, Mel Sturgess. He parked the car, leaped out, and peeled open the box to see the glassy eyes of a six-point buck staring back at him. Leaving the remainder of his belongings in the car, Hunter carried the deer head up the stairs and through the door. In short order, using a hammer and mounting kit he found in the adjoining warehouse, he placed the deer head in the center of the main wall in the living room, facing his brown leather lounge chair that arrived the day before.

Hunter then did something he was not able to do since he left in shame from Dallas, Texas and arrived in Cleveland. He sat down in the lounge chair and felt the stuffing mold to his body. Flipping out the footrest and easing the chair back, he fell asleep in moments.

*     *     *

Within days Hunter's apartment filled with various items: Zita bought him a boot-shaped lamp she found at a yard sale. His deputies chipped in to buy him a set of wine glasses engraved with his initials, *H H.* Deputy Chan brought him a small CD player and a collection of CD's: *Best Blues Hits from the Mississippi Delta*, which included Goldie Parson's song. His big surprise was a gift from Shannon--a woolen throw with ducks and deer figures on a dark brown background. Her message said, *Stay warm. My love. Shannon.*

Hunter also received his strangest gift from his newest deputy, Carlton Newman. Mayor Willis, who was also re-elected, called him the day after the election, speaking on behalf of Carlton. "Sheriff," said the mayor, "Can you give him a job in your office on a trial basis? I will understand if it doesn't work out, but the kid is crazy smart. I know his social skills need some work, but if someone will just give him a chance, I think he'll come around." When Carlton gave him a box of bow ties as a housewarming gift, Hunter faked a smile and was reminded of what he signed up for.

One of the larger items Hunter needed appeared one morning as he washed his hands in the kitchen sink. Through the window sporting burlap curtains with red checkered trim—

another yard sale find from Zita that she bragged about—he spotted the rustic brown leather sofa he ordered in the back of a delivery truck headed down the street towards his apartment. He pulled on his boots, rushed out the door, and down the stairs, and waved at the driver as he turned onto the street. He directed them to the rear of the building to the old loading elevator.

The truck backed up to the building and as he walked to the back entrance, he noticed two delivery boxes by the front door of the first floor apartment. *V must be coming home soon,* He thought. Hunter opened the loading dock doors, lowered the freight elevator, then helped the delivery men load the couch onto its wooden flatbed.

Everyone jumped as a black streak of fur darted under the couch as it lifted off the ground to the second floor. "Damn! I knew there was a cat!" Hunter bent over to stare under the couch. Two bright green eyes glared back at him. "I saw it hanging around before. I'll get rid of it. Here, Kitty, Kitty," he called out but a hiss was the only response.

"Whew! He was fast!" stated one of the delivery men. "Catching that one won't be easy." When they got to the top and the elevator stopped, the black kitten scrambled off the freight elevator and into the warehouse before they could catch it. Fluffy with thick black fur and a white-tipped nose and paws, like a tuxedo, the cat was lost amongst the various art items before Hunter could determine anything else about it. As it dashed between the art canvases, he yelled, "If you think you're coming into my new house, cat, you're wrong!"

"Hey man, we have another delivery. We don't have time to chase your cat," said the other delivery man.

"It's not my cat!" Hunter replied as he tried to see where the kitten scampered. Pushing the thoughts of the cat to the side, he guided the men into his apartment. In short order, the new couch was placed against the wall under the designer deer head, and the delivery men were promptly tipped.

Hunter pointed to the cat that had sneaked past them into the apartment. "Shoo!" he yelled at it. His command went unheeded.

"Good luck with the cat! That rascal seems determined!" said one of the men as they loaded into the truck and drove away.

Hunter could swear he heard the kitten hiss again as he walked back into his apartment to call Zita for advice. He was not a cat person; he would choose a red tick coonhound over a puff ball of a cat any day. He was at a loss of what to do.

A call to Zita's number found her unavailable, so he sent her a text. *Cat got into the warehouse. Need help getting him out.*

An unexpected shuffle of noise caused Hunter to glance up and reach for the rifle he kept behind the front door. To his surprise, he saw the black and white kitten sitting calmly on his lounge chair, watching his every move. The ball of fluff eyed him while scratching the leather footrest.

"Get out of my chair!" Hunter swatted at the creature causing it to scamper across the beige carpet and crouched in a corner in a defense mode, hissing and meowing, daring him to come nearer. Not intimidated, Hunter tried to grab it by the nape of its neck. The cat got revenge. It ended up clawing deeply as it ran up his outreached arm, vaulted through the air and, to the surprise of both Hunter and the kitten, landed on the newly installed deer head hanging on the wall.

Hunter snarled at the kitten through gritted teeth. "Just wait till I get my hands on you; I'll get my broom and get you out of here and then I'm going to take you to the city pound."

When Hunter returned with the broom, the kitten had managed to get down from its perch. He found it curled up in the corner of the new couch on the blanket Shannon had given him. The fire-eater he'd just dealt with now looked weak and helpless.

The kitten didn't resist when Hunter gathered it into his arms with the protection of a large towel he'd retrieved from the bathroom. He cringed when one of the skinny creature's fleas bit his hand. He scratched its ears as it hissed once more, but then rested its head in the crook of Hunter's arm. "Poor little fellow. Looks like you're sick. I'm going to take you to the vet and see what's wrong. They'll fix you up. But don't get too comfortable. You're not going to stay here. I don't have time for a pet. Maybe the vet can find you a good home."

Hunter sent a text to Zita, updating her on the situation. *The cat is sick. Taking it to the vet.*

She texted him back, *Good idea.*

Like everything else in Cleveland, the vet's office was an easy two block drive from his apartment. He kept telling the vet's assistant he wanted to just drop it off and let them find it a home, but no one listened. Hunter found himself in a room in the back, the cat still wrapped up in a towel waiting for the vet to arrive.

Minutes later the vet came in, a sweet, bubbly young woman with purple hair, and Hunter learned the kitten was about ten weeks old, increasingly vocal as he worked up the strength to squirm and hiss and, according to the vet, a male. As it turned out, nobody wanted a sick cat, or even one Hunter had spent $300.00 on for treatment and antibiotics. He even got on the list to have the kitten neutered in two weeks.

Hunter took the black bundle back to his apartment and left him curled up on the bathroom rug to go shopping. He soon returned home with a litter box, a forty-pound bag of litter and a variety of cat food. The vet said it was important for the kitten to put on weight. Hunter discovered the cat ate the food it liked, the most expensive brands, and turned up its nose at other food, the least expensive ones. The same was true with litter. It only used the litter box if the litter in it met his approval, otherwise an "accident" happened in Hunter's bathroom.

The fearless kitten strolled across the countertops and the kitchen table at its leisure and escaped every time Hunter tried to chase it out of the bedroom. One day, it ran into the bathroom and licked the nurdle Hunter had just put on his toothbrush, the mint flavor causing the kitten's little nose to wrinkle. He chased it back into the bedroom and it hopped onto his pillow with an innocent "Meow." The pitiful cry caused Hunter's anger to subside, but the kitten didn't let Hunter come close. It still scampered away when he approached. Although the fluffy boy refused to be petted, he would appear right beside Hunter's head on the bed when he awoke in the mornings.

Hunter made an announcement to Zita one day while she was at his place, the kitten curled beside her. "I finally have a name for that damned cat," he said. "It's King. He rules my domain, so he may as well get the title."

Zita leaned back and chuckled. "It fits. Yep. Maybe you should call him King George, III. It suits a tyrant in charge. You picked a good one for this pet. Ha, people around here will think he's named for B. B. King."

Hunter pointed to King as the cat stretched out on the couch. "He's aware we're talking about him, but he's too comfortable to care."

"If people want to think he's named for B. B. King, let them. B. B. was a powerful figure as a blues singer. Bet he was in charge of lots of things, too. Yeah, like this King, B. B. ruled his domain."

"Guess what, Hunter? Maybe you're lucky King even lets you live in *his* house." Zita laughed while scratching the cat behind its ear.

Hunter had to laugh, too. "Come to think of it, I didn't even choose that cat; it chose me. Wrong order. Doesn't that damn animal realize I am the highest-ranking police official in thiscounty?"

Zita shrugged. "I reckon not. Just how do you plan to enforce your authority?"

He didn't even try to answer that question.

# Chapter 2

Two weeks later Hunter brought King to the office resting in his shiny new cat carrier, a small white paw and pink toes resting on its bars. Drowsy from his spaying and shots, King snored intermittently. Hunter needed to keep an eye on King as he recovered, but he also had to be at work. His only option was to bring King to the station. As Hunter placed the carrier on the floor behind his desk, the phone jingled. He answered the call and, out of habit, put it on speaker while he rearranged papers. Zita walked in and he motioned her to take a seat as he glanced down at King still sleeping in the carrier.

A familiar voice boomed out, "Harley Hunter, you there? This is Roy Reed, from your old stomping ground. You haven't forgotten me, I hope. How're you doing over in hick town, ha, ha? Bet you miss all the excitement in Dallas since you're in dullsville."

"Hey, Roy, I'm here. Got my deputy, Officer Rocconi, here too. Things are better and she can vouch for me. How are you? Still busy fighting crime in the big city?"

Used to similar jokes, Zita rolled her eyes. But Hunter now saw Cleveland as his town and felt protective about it. "Cleveland's not as calm as you might think. Believe it or not, things here have been chaotic. We had bones wash up along a local river recently. You heard of that sixty years-old missing blues singer case–Goldie Parsons? Have you ever dealt with anything like that?"

"Amazing! In Cleveland, Mississippi? Now that's a cold case. Who's the singer again?"

"Goldie Parsons—he made one record: a smash hit that made him famous. Still being played."

"Yeah, I do know the name! Song's called *Reelin' Feelin'*, right?"

"Right. You must be a Mississippi Delta Blue's fan. Do you know Goldie Parsons' granddaughter lives in Cleveland?"

Deputy Carlton walked into the room and blurted out, "Don't forget B. B. King, he is also from here. His guitars were all named Lucille and he had their f holes removed to reduce feedback. He said, 'My guitar strings speak to the world.' He once went into a burning building to retrieve his Gibson. After that…"

Through gritted teeth, Hunter ordered Carlton out of the room before he could continue his showing off. Then he resumed his phone conversation, saying, "Sorry for the interruption by my know-it-all deputy. He's the mayor's nephew. Nepotism. That's how he got the job."

"No problem. There's one of those in every crowd. Interesting; I'd like to meet Parsons' granddaughter sometime. I love B. B. King and his famous Lucilles."

King stirred in his carrier at the mention of his name, and Hunter checked to see if he was okay. The puff ball shifted a little but continued sleeping.

Roy continued, "Got a record collection, but not that one. I do have it on a CD. I have got to pay you a visit soon." He cleared his throat. "Hunter, I hate to tell you this, but this call isn't just social. I know it's a touchy subject with you, but it's about your last case in Dallas—the one we dubbed the Dallas Devil. You know the one where you were asked to…you know. When you left, the missing children cases stopped. We were hoping it was over, but he's at it again. A few weeks ago, he took a white kid on her walk to school, snatched her and forced her into his van. This is the part that is interesting: her name is Heather Harley. You and I both know you do not have any living family here, but the kidnapper obviously didn't. According to Heather, the kidnapper never said a word. He had an old school tape recorder and it kept repeating, 'tell Hunter Harley he is next.'" A chill ran down Hunter's spine.

Hunter could hear the relief in Roy's voice when he said, "That ten-year-old outwitted the jerk. He took her to a convenience store and let her go to the bathroom. She unscrewed the toilet seat lid, used it to block the stall door, and started yelling for help. The manager heard her on the other side of the wall, called the police and the kidnapper took off. We caught them on the gas station security camera, but the image is too blurry. We did get the tag number from the van; a witness wrote it down. It was stolen hours before he picked up the girl. We found it dumped in Lake Tawakoni State Park. He ran it into the water. No prints."

Zita chewed on her bottom lip as she met Harley's gaze. He leaned back in his chair but didn't want to show any emotion in front of her. He struggled not to squirm.

Roy continued but his voice was whispery, "Two days ago we got a letter with terrible handwriting, but we managed to read it. I wanted to call you immediately, but the department head didn't want to be bothered, didn't think it was real. I recognized the handwriting immediately. You know those two dead children we found with the note from the murderer and missing piece of hair? It was the same! He claimed that he knew where you were and he's coming after you. It's postmarked from Memphis a week ago, so I think he could already be in Cleveland. I had to warn you, Harley. Uh, oh, gotta go." Harley could hear Roy being questioned before he hung up the phone.

When the call ended, Zita hopped out of her chair. "What the Hell is he talking about? Why didn't you tell us about this? It's dangerous having a person like this in Cleveland. What if he goes after one of our kids?"

"Calm down, Zita." He held up a palm toward her. "Sit back down and let me tell you the rest of the story. You see, I almost caught that devil…well, I thought I had. When Jenny Stein, that so-called journalist, started writing about my investigation, making up stuff, the crazy person committing these crimes focused on me." He sighed. "Unfortunately, I got the wrong guy; he was a no-good son-of-a-gun, but not the Dallas Devil.  Everything matched, except finding evidence of hair collected from the victims, the Devil's marker, this man was the one…I thought. He was a drug dealer, and he was in the right places at the right times. He also had a long arrest record, but a solid witness came forward while he sat in jail waiting for his trial. The mistake and Jenny Stein's false reporting was enough to turn the Dallas Police Department against me.  I don't blame them; I was a mess at the time since my Mamma died. That's why I left Dallas—it was resign or be fired. I still feel terrible about it but catching the Devil might make something right."

He stood in front of Zita, chair squeaking as it pushed back. "I've been in worse situations. If the Dallas Devil is here to get me, it'll be my chance to grab him."

"If he doesn't get you first." She stood and shook her finger at him. "I have watched enough big city murder documentaries to know this can turn bad fast. We have a small force here. It could be hard to back you up. Sounds like this is a ruthless criminal."

"He's capable of anything, a serial killer with an agenda, but we can't prove it—yet. The one thing so far that is consistent between all the cases is a lock of hair missing from every victim." *An image of a pair of manicure scissors flashed through his brain. A picture of something he'd entirely forgotten. But where had he seen them?* Hunter stared into space but couldn't force anything else from his memory.

Zita again met Hunter's gaze, "Clearly, we are dealing with a psychopath. He's ready to take things a step farther. It looks like you are the prey this time, Hunter."

"I won't let that happen." He forgot the manicure scissors as his thoughts became more personal. *Damn, it thrills me to see that fire in her eyes.*

Zita got close and looked up into her boss's face, frowning when a small smile cracked his lips. "You're big and strong, but are you sure you can stop him?" She picked up her tablet, looked again at Hunter, and walked out. Confused at this new bit of information, she went back to her office to think things out.

After she left, Hunter closed his office door and stared out the window at citizens walking down the street, oblivious to dangers lurking in the shadows. Little did they suspect what might await around the corner. He stared at dark clouds high in the sky looking like bruises and viewed them as ominous symbols of pending danger.

"No," he whispered through clenched teeth, "the truth is I'm not sure I can protect myself, or others, from that devil." He banged the desk with his fist. "But I'll sure as hell do my damnedest, even if I die trying."

*     *     *

Hunter had left his office at two p.m. to take King to his home. Fully awake, the kitten had managed to scoot the crate close enough to scratch Hunter's ankle to get attention. Hunter informed Zita he was taking "his highness" home before he drew any more blood. Zita assured him she'd watch things till the night shift arrived.

From a window, Zita watched Hunter ease the jiggling cat carrier into the passenger seat. He paused to pull a tissue from his back pocket to wrap a newly acquired scratch. Getting into the driver's seat, he backed  his patrol car onto the street.

Zita stared at the hole she'd bitten in the Reuben sandwich she brought for lunch but ended up eating it for supper. It reminded her of other holes in her life. Her thoughts wandered back to Hunter and she felt protective of him. He was a tough, no nonsense type of man, but knowing someone was trying to endanger his life made her want to do something, anything, to help.

She glanced at the monitor resting on her standing desk and the folder containing files of the case she should be working on. Unlike Hunter, who tried to keep things in the proper place on his desk, hers was covered with stacks of paper, small plastic bags containing evidence from a case she was processing and, atop it all, the brown bag which had contained her lunch.

Curiosity about Hunter's previous life consumed her. What else had happened in Dallas? How many children had suffered irreparable damage that changed their lives forever at the hands of that evil monster? She shuddered. How horrible that two innocent, vulnerable children died at the hands of the murderer. How could Hunter fend off such a terrible person here in Cleveland? She was determined to not let him face this killer alone, but to do so she needed to know more.

Taking a second bite of her sandwich, Zita mulled over the situation. She knew this was only the beginning, the edge of the sword. She glanced towards Hunter's office door at his empty chair. Should she tell her boss she was snooping? He was sensitive about the situation, but he shared the story with her because she happened to be in the room when Roy called. Maybe she needed to respect his space and chew on this for a while.

Zita smiled at the pun as she savored the flavor of corned beef and sauerkraut. It diverted her attention, but only for a moment. Her thoughts returned to digging into Hunter's past. Fighting curiosity was useless; she had to find out what she could no matter what he thought.

She stuck the rest of her sandwich back into a baggie, put it in the brown bag and moved it to the top of another pile of papers. Then she pulled her tablet from between the stack of folders. She could research what she needed on it and hide it if Hunter happened to walk back to the office.

Her first search was a simple one, only the "Dallas Devil." The top of the search engine brought up the numerous articles written by Jenny Stein. From the articles Zita gathered this was the first serial killer case in Dallas since Charles Fredrick Albright, known as the Eyeball Killer.

In addition, even after all this time, the Dallas Police Department did not have any idea of the identity of the suspect. She clicked on other articles and write ups not written by Jenny that crossed her screen to try to get a perspective. Tightening every muscle in her body, Zita braced herself for any gory details she might unveil.

The earliest possible case happened about four years ago to a six-year-old black girl named Janice Courtney. Old missing persons' flyers flashed across her tablet screen with the school picture of the little girl's face in the center. The short description below the photo stated she was with her older brother, who left her for a moment, but when he returned, she was gone without a trace.

The articles that followed indicated the Dallas PD and her family anticipated the worst. Strangely, Stein was not the author of any of those early articles. Then the *Dallas Morning Times* reported a miracle happened, Janice appeared on the front porch of her home two weeks later. Her small body was emaciated, and she was filthy. She wore the same clothes she disappeared in. She refused to talk to anyone and cringed at any physical contact. She clammed up about the time she was missing. Zita made a fist. *She must have been so frightened.*

Zita stared at the screen of her tablet, engrossed in what she was reading, and shaking her head. When a photo of Jenny flashed across her screen, she heard a noise and looked up. Hunter stood in front of her desk.

Startled, she said, "Hey, you're back. I…"

"Forgot my cell phone."

Zita could tell from his expression he knew what she was doing. His lips tightened into a straight line as he leaned over her stack of papers to see the tablet screen with a photo of Jenny, showing her solemn expression. Zita met his green eyes and saw the transition of emotions: anger, irritation, confusion and, finally, acceptance. Hunter's head dropped to his chest. He pulled up the old, uncomfortable wooden office chair, the one she used when interrogating petty criminals, and sat down next to Zita. Springs creaked as Hunter leaned forward, resting his elbows on his knees, "I guess it's time to come clean."

Zita kept silent as Hunter recalled the story. He pointed to the tablet screen and said he was ecstatic when Janice's parents called two weeks after she went missing saying their child appeared. They rushed her to the Methodist Emergency Room. They examined her but found no serious injuries, so they discharged her.

Hunter shook his head. "I rushed to the hospital as soon as I found out. That brave little girl refused to talk, but we discovered one clue–two plaits of her hair were cut off. He even took the hair ties that matched. Her mother said they had blue plastic flowers attached.  The investigation got a little help, though. A neighbor walking his dog on their street came forward. He was so far away when it happened, he wasn't sure what he saw. He said a man wearing blue Jeans, and a black jacket with a hoodie picked up what appeared to be a small child and put her into a white van. Since they had no other leads on the perpetrator of the crime, there was nothing they could do.

Hunter's eyes clouded. "Zita, I hated seeing that little girl suffering through that examination in the hospital. No child should go through something like this. I'm glad she was okay. At the time, we were not sure what type of person we were dealing with. I was made the lead on this case, and failure wasn't an option. When they found the bodies of those two other children after Janice, I was devastated. I could see his murder pattern progressing from kidnapping to murder, but I couldn't stop him. I failed."

"Hunter," she rested a hand on his shoulder, "our job is not an easy one. We deal with the ugly things of the world, so others do not have to. We see the seedy side of life. But know this, I care about you and we all want to help you if you will let us. You do not have to carry this load alone."

Hunter's green eyes met her brown ones and he nodded, a single tear running down his cheek.

From the corner of her eye, Zita saw a figure standing behind her. Then she noticed Carlton back out of the room and tiptoe toward his office. She did not point out his presence to her boss.

# Chapter 3

Hunter remembered his mother, Ruby, telling him more than once, "Son, sometimes you have to show people you care about them, instead of just telling them." He decided one way to do this would be to have a real Texas themed Thanksgiving meal in honor of the family no longer with him and his newly formed family in Cleveland. He had a choice, worry if the Devil was in Cleveland or keep his mind busy with other things until he knew for sure. He was careful, though. He paid attention to his surroundings, requested his officers to keep an eye out for anything unusual and kept his gun on him at all times.

When he moved to Cleveland, the lack of a kitchen at the Pink Palace gave people the impression he did not know how to cook. Hunter wanted to surprise everyone with what he could do. He studied the manual that came with his Erik range with the built-in grill. Using that range honed his skills in the kitchen, along with his expertise in cooking. Now his skills weren't limited to grilling. His attempt at preparing various dishes, including catfish, provided lush scrapes for King to enjoy as he grew. As a result, his skinny black tail had formed into a fluffy one topped with a white tip on the end.

Hunter was prepared for this Thanksgiving party, the first holiday he'd had off since he moved to Cleveland. He gathered the best ingredients and mentally checked his menu.

He'd baked a turkey, but he also bought steaks. While the grill heated, his marinated steaks were seasoned and ready to grill. For appetizers, he put dabs of peanut butter on top of Waverly wafers wrapped in a strip of bacon on a cookie sheet and baked them in the oven. He called them Waverly treats. Corn in the husks went into the microwave. When he closed the kitchen door, he saw two golden eyes staring back at him, seeking a piece. "Sorry King, you don't get to try this meal. Maybe after the party."

Later, when the corn was done, Hunter chopped off the ends and squeezed them to clear all the husks and silk. Next, he cooked frozen chopped spinach, drained it, and mixed it with softened cream cheese, adding a couple of cans of cream of mushroom soup. As he topped it with frozen onion rings, he chuckled. He'd served this many times and it always fooled his guests. Nobody would believe it was spinach. But they always knew what it was when he served potato salad dosed with a secret ingredient. A huge bowl of his specialty chilled in the refrigerator along with beer and a bottle of Merlot on its door shelves.

Sticking to his theme, he hung a Texas state flag on his small outdoor porch and sipped his coffee as he watched it wave in the wind from the kitchen window. Hunter was still searching for a kitchen table to fit his large space but found a massive handmade table in the storage area next to his apartment to use temporarily. V had not returned yet, but he didn't think he would mind.  He dragged the table into his space and put a thick red tablecloth on top to protect the finish.

Hunter unwrapped Ruby's everyday use China plates, a set of seven covered with bluebonnets, and placed them with matching napkins on the handmade kitchen table. He also unwrapped the glasses with the single gold stars on the side and put one at each place setting. He smiled as he opened the silverware box and placed his mother's sterling silverware on either side of each plate. It had been stashed away but now he wanted to use it. *Mom would be proud. She always used to say silverware is made for using. At home, we did use it every day.*

Wearing a Thanksgiving sweater, complete with a large turkey on the front, Zita arrived just as Hunter placed the steaks on the grill and set the timer. "Wow!" she exclaimed as she glanced around. "You're really putting on a show." She walked over to a side table, lifted the lid of a cake dish, and took a sniff. "Yummy, smells like pound cake."

"It is. An old family recipe, as they say." He adjusted a control on the cooktop to simmer. "When you're baking with an Erik appliance, it's hard to fail. It's a part of the secret of good cooking."

"I'm not a very good cook. You reckon a new stove would help?" Zita winked at him as she walked over to the kitchen window. "Get ready, Shannon and the kids are almost here."

"What? Okay. Have you met the kids yet? Anything I need to know?"

Before Zita could answer, a knock on his door interrupted. When he opened it, Shannon stood there, dressed much more casually than the last time he saw her, in Jeans and a bright yellow T-shirt, but still polished. She held the hands of her two adopted children. "Hi, Hunter. It's been forever! Thank you for inviting us! Here are my two new charges." She pointed left. "This is Karla," and then right, "And this is Charles." She directed the children inside and then whispered to Hunter,

"Charles is rambunctious, but don't worry, I'll keep him under control."

Hunter then felt a slight tug on the back of his shirt. He looked down at the tow-headed freckle-faced boy, who announced, "I'm ten, and she's six." Karla, a copy of her brother but with darker features, peeked from behind and glanced up at Hunter. She gave a sweet smile when Charles mentioned her.

Hunter rumpled Charles' hair, and then bent over to offer a handshake to Karla. She reached from behind her brother, rested her hand in Hunter's, and shook it once before pulling away. "Good to meet you, young lady." He pointed to King sitting on the back of the couch. "You see that half-grown puff ball over there? His name is King. If you sit quietly on the couch, he may choose to climb in your lap, but he has to choose, okay? If you rush him, he may scratch you."

"Yes, sir." said Charles as Karla nodded.

As the guests eyed the way the kitchen was set up and the appealing smells from the food, Shannon whistled and commented, "You're renting this place from the famous artist, V, whose store faces Main street, and he lives downstairs, right?" She didn't wait for a reply; she just kept glancing around. "This place is something else. The carving on the front door is amazing." She pointed to the table. "I bet V made that. I can see his style on the legs. Have you met him yet? is work is internationally known! I saw it all over D. C."

Hunter nodded. "I've seen V around, but he has been out of town since I rented this place. So, he's famous, huh? That explains all the strange things stored in this building. I saw V once in passing when I first moved here but haven't had a chance to talk with him. I got a call from his lawyer in Memphis and it looks like he is coming back here next week."

Shannon continued, "How exciting and the timing couldn't be better. You'll never guess what I did. You know we are renovating the Tollar Plantation house, right? Some of the work is done by professionals, but I am working on the inside, myself. I got tired and took a break from scraping paint off the living room wall at the homeplace. I had time to go into V's store yesterday. I was roaming around inside and guess what I saw? There it was! An amazing guitar-shaped statute constructed of scraps of metal, parts of a wagon wheel, and of old cars. He makes magic! It's an outstanding piece!"

"I rushed to the front desk and talked to the store manager and offered to buy it. I told him it would be perfect for Goldie's tombstone if it were bronzed, so it would hold up in the weather. Can you believe he refused my generous offer? If I can talk to V, himself, then I am sure I can convince him. You know, lots of things in his shop were marked 'Not for sale.' Kind of odd, but typical of artists. Everyone says V is quite a character."

Hunter realized he missed a key part of the conversation, "Wait, tombstone for Goldie? What are you planning?"

"We can work out the details later, but I can now bury my mother, grandmother and Goldie together at the Tollar Plantation. It wasn't easy, but I got the paperwork cleared. Everyone's remains are now here in town at the funeral home. I want this over with as fast as possible." Shannon told Hunter.

Before Hunter could respond, another knock came. This time, the guest was Carlton, wearing a white shirt and tie. So, this nerd wouldn't dress in a weird fashion, Hunter had to specifically tell Carlton not to wear his uniform nor a suit. He could see Carlton hesitate at the door, looking like he wondered what to do next, but the new deputy needed to be stretched a little and this was as good a time as any. Hunter said, "Come in, Carlton. Good to see you away from work."

Seconds later Chan, dressed in jeans and a polo shirt, sauntered in without knocking. "Hope I'm not late. Man, it sure smells good. You must have a feast."

Everyone sat around in the living room making small talk until Hunter announced dinner was ready. Most of the guests knew each other. The only one everyone didn't really know was Shannon and her two children. Carlton, true to his style, eyed the two kids and remarked to Shannon, "I didn't know you were married."

Shannon smiled. "I'm not, never have been." When she didn't explain these weren't her children by birth, Carlton's eyes opened wide.

To change the subject, grinning, Hunter offered everyone a drink. All asked for beer, but when Hunter passed out bottles, only Carlton requested a glass. The two kids enjoyed cold sodas from the fridge.

"By the way," Shannon said, "Tippiny sent her thanks for the invitation and her best wishes. That was nice of you to ask her. She still misses living here with her mom, Mama Cheche. I think she misses Cleveland, too. She's so busy in D. C. at her new job that she couldn't get away in time. She is coming for my family's memorial service."

The oven timer sounded. Hunter retrieved the wafers, placed them onto a dish and passed it around. The kids ate three each and Shannon commented, "These are delicious. What a tasty combination."

Carlton didn't try them. "I'm allergic to peanuts," he said, waving them off.

When Hunter returned to the kitchen to get the turkey, he noticed his cell phone blinking. He got a text message. He took a minute to stir the potatoes, then checked the message. His heart dropped.  It was from Roy in Dallas: *I got a call on the Texas Crime Stoppers anonymous phone line. This person claims to be the Dallas Devil and knows your address. Just wanted to warn you. He's trying to scare you. Take care, old buddy.*

Hunter slammed the phone on the counter and noticed Zita looking towards him. He saw her mouthing the words, *You okay?*

He nodded. Slicing the turkey, he placed it on a platter to carry it to the dining area. *Damn it, I'm not going to let this idiot ruin my party. We've got four of us deputies here. If anything happens, we'll handle it.* Hunter walked back to his guests with a smile on his face and offered to replenish their drinks. "I'll have more Coke, and so will my sister," Charles piped up.

Hunter complied, finding it touching that the boy spoke for his sister. Then he announced that the steaks were ready and invited his guests to come to the table where he'd placed all the serving dishes with assistance from Zita.

"I can only eat well done meat," Carlton stared at the platter of steaks, poking one with the serving fork.

"I was just getting ready to tell you that the ones on the left are medium rare. The others are almost well-done. My grill has less heat on one side."

Carlton pointed to a steak a bit larger than the rest. "Could you put that one back on the grill for three minutes?"

Hunter bit his tongue as he complied with the request. He looked at Zita rolling her eyes when Carlton set the timer. Everyone else sat down to eat. When Carlton's steak was done, Hunter let him get it himself.

As Carlton headed back to the table, he screeched. Then he kicked his leg sideways. Zita burst out laughing when she saw

King scampering away and then turning to hiss at a shaking Carlton.

"That cat was about to attack me," Carlton complained.

Zita rose, went to the kitten and petted it. "It's okay, King." She then said, "Carlton, he only wanted a treat."

The rest of the guests and the host laughed. In a huff, Carlton plopped into a chair at the table. "Well, a damn cat isn't going to spoil my dinner. Good thing it didn't make me drop my plate. I'd have…."

Stares stopped him in mid-sentence. Ignoring them, he stuffed steak and then turkey into his mouth. When Hunter made a toast to "Good friends and coworkers" to ease the tension, Carlton didn't raise his glass.

While the adults chatted, Charles and Karla filled their plates and ate with zest, gobbling their food. Carlton revived and took the floor. "Shannon, Goldie Parsons was your grandfather, right? I heard people talking about a movie. I saw a new coat of paint on the old Tollar Plantation, is that what is going on out there? They say all they need is funding. They're looking for a philanderer. Any of you know one?"

When everyone laughed, Hunter said, "Don't you mean a philanthropist, Carlton?" It was the fourth time he'd heard Carlton use a malapropism. *The guy's not stupid, but he's not near as smart as he thinks he is.* He sucked in his cheek. *Worse yet, he has terrible social skills.*

Carlton arched his back. "Of course, I was just making a joke." His face reddened.

Then young Charles unknowingly saved face for Carlton by changing the subject. "What's for dessert?" he blurted out, ignoring Shannon's glare.

"How do you like cake and ice cream?" Hunter rose and cut the cake on the counter while Zita brought out the ice cream and dessert plates. On the way, she had a dab ready to drop into King's bowl but stopped midair. *Oh, no, I read where lots of cats are lactose intolerant. I won't take a chance.* She put the ice cream on a guest's plate instead before placing scoops on other guests' plates.

"Yuk! That cake's not chocolate," Charles complained, shoving aside the plate he was handed with a slice of cake on it. "Don't eat it," he ordered his sister.

"Charles!" Shannon called out to the boy sitting beside her. "That's not polite. Now say you're sorry to Sheriff Hunter."

Charles stuck out a lip. "I'm not sorry. I only like chocolate…"

Shannon grabbed the child's arm and pulled his face close to hers. "Young man, you will apologize, or I'll take care of you when we get home."

Charles hung his head. "I'm, er, I'm-I'm sorry."

"That's okay, Charles. I like chocolate myself," Hunter chimed in. "And we do have chocolate ice cream."

Zita produced a carton and dropped a couple of scoops of chocolate ice cream on top of the cake on the boy's plate. Charles scraped the ice cream aside. "I don't like it touching." Seeing Shannon's frown, Charles said, "Sorry," this time without being prompted. Hunter eyed the exchange. He hoped he never got one of those looks from Shannon.

The incident was over, but another began for Hunter when his cell phone rang on the counter. He got up and answered it without looking at the screen and said, "Hello."

All he heard were guttural sounds. Was this a prank call?

Turning his back to his guests, he exited the room, went to his bedroom, and closed the door. "Who is this? You know I am a police officer? This prank call could get you a jail sentence." he blurted out in a hurried voice.

Just as he moved the phone from his ear a deep raspy voice announced: "I know where you are. How did you like the voodoo dust I put all over your car? Going crazy yet?" Click.

Hunter looked to see the number of the last caller. It was an unknown one, but Hunter knew who it was. He went into the bathroom and splashed water on his face in an effort to compose himself. It didn't work. He looked into the mirror. *Hunter Harley, don't let this get to you. Go back to your guests.*" He walked out of the room bearing a forced smile.

The rest of the afternoon, he sat around and listened to the small talk of his guests, but kept checking outside the windows. It got his attention when Shannon said, "There's something odd about the Tollar Plantation that gives me an eerie feeling. I know all old houses make strange noises, but it gives me the creeps late at night. Makes me wonder if folks around here are right when they say houses become haunted if someone dies in one. You know, my great-grandmother died in this house."

"According to local folklore," Zita added, "If a person dies and leaves money buried, so that nobody knows where it is, they say his spirit will come back, and the color of the spirit is red. Seen anything red around the place lately?"

Shannon's eyes grew wide as she stared at Hunter for his response. But he just shrugged. "Don't ask me. I'm not a native of Cleveland. I'm just an old-fashioned Texas lawman."

King strutted over and stopped in front of his owner, seeking his promised leftovers. "Uh, oh. The master is hungry."

Hunter didn't want to speculate about those kinds of things around here. Tending to his pet gave him an out for further comments.

When he placed bits of turkey and a spoonful of potatoes into King's bowl, Carlton piped up. "No need to give him anything sweet. Cats can't experience the taste." Before Hunter could say he knew that Carlton switched subjects by bumbling out a riddle. Hunter listened and he even managed a chuckle at Carlton's joke about how a visitor to the Garden of Eden could recognize Adam and Eve. Chin held high Carlton flaunted his knowledge that their missing "Navys" gave them away. Everyone laughed more at his misstatement of "navels" than at the joke. But Carlton was too obtuse to realize that.

Everyone worked together to clean up the kitchen and wrap up the leftovers. Hunter was grateful for the help, but he was relieved when the last guest, Carlton, left. He locked the door, got the pistol he'd locked up while children were in the house, and plopped down into his lounge chair, pondering over what that call meant. He knew that it was from the Dallas Devil and he was officially in town. What his next move should be was in doubt. It only took a few minutes to make him realize there wasn't much he could do at this point. The Dallas Devil put Hunter into a vulnerable position. Who or what could he turn to?

# Chapter 4

Hunter sat in his recliner when everyone left and stared at the walls to let his nerves settle. The phone call triggered something in the recesses of his memory. It was a person he'd tried to put out of his mind as non-existent: the old lady in Janice's dream. He had to admit any reference to Mama Cheche had given him pause, but he'd hidden his emotions and hadn't reacted. So, nobody knew anything about his thoughts of a connection, if there was one. Though he couldn't deny the possibility, Hunter dismissed any Mojo and forced the word *superstitious* into his brain anytime he had such thoughts. It was merely a coincidence. Shaking his head to clear it, he forced his thoughts to be sensible. He refused to believe in the Mojo.

Cora Thompson had asked Janice if she saw anything unusual. The child bit the corner of her lip and picked at a frayed edge of her blue dress. Her small fingernails were chewed raw, "You won't believe me if I tell you."

"Yes, we will." Cora patted the child's hand.

Hunter nodded agreement when Janice glanced towards him, but kept silent.

Janice said in a whispery voice that both Karla and Hunter had to lean in to hear clearly, "One night I had a dream of an old lady."

Cora's eyes widened. "What lady? You didn't mention her before."

Janice shrugged. "What did she look like?"

"She was black, but her skin was not as dark as mine. Her hair was nice and white, and she had something like an angel's thing on top of her head."

"You mean a halo," Cora offered.

Janice bobbed her head. "She didn't say anything. She just held up her hand like she was pointing to heaven."

Hunter recalled how his muscles had tightened, how he thought of Mama Cheche and the mojo. Had this little girl heard some wild story and repeated it? Was she making up this dream? He remembered how confusing her words were back then, but he'd restrained himself.

When Janice cocked her head, Hunter saw she was missing two plaits. Her mother had combed it down the best she could, but short hair curled tight next to her scalp. She picked at her dress again. "I thought the lady in my dream was an angel. Mama said to pray to Jesus when I didn't understand things. I prayed when I woke up."

Hunter's Adam's apple bobbed as he swallowed hard, as he listened to the child's report: "Then the man screamed at me when I said I dreamed about an angel. He told me angels don't exist and to shut up. I didn't believe him."

Was Mama somehow coming into this child's dreams? A chill ran down Hunter's spine.

As if triggered by those thoughts, Hunter's phone rang again. It was Levenia calling from the cafe. "Something weird just happened, Hunter," she said. "The place is full of people, you know, those who don't want to cook for Thanksgiving? You know Missy? Donna's daughter?  She left her phone on the table you usually sit at when she went to the restroom. When she came back, it was gone. She asked me about it and we looked all over- -on the floor, in the restroom, and she dumped everything out of her purse. It was nowhere to be found. We went outside to check her car and when we came back to the table, it was in the chair she'd been sitting in.  I had to call you."

"I'm glad you did. Is Missy still there? Did you notice anyone suspicious in the diner or outside?"

"No, she left with her phone. I recall seeing one young guy with a cap pulled down sitting at a corner table. He was fiddling with his phone; one of those fancy iPhones. Before I could take his order, he was gone. In a breathy voice she added, "We have a small blues band playing music on the front porch for tips.  I asked them if they saw anything, but only one noticed anything suspicious."

"What did he say?"

"Not much. Just that he saw a man about twenty go into the diner a short while before."

*Damn! I don't think that's my guy. I have him pegged as being middle aged. But what if...?* "Did he remember what he looked like? How was he dressed? If he had a weapon?"

"He said he was short, dark-haired, and clean shaven. He thinks he had on jeans and expensive sneakers, but he didn't seem sure. Wait a minute, I see Zita driving in. You know that is one good woman. She is always checking on me."

"Hey, don't say…" she had put the phone down before Hunter could stop her from telling Zita what happened.

The next voice on the line was Zita's, "Hunter could that be the call you got during the party? Are you ok?"

"I am. That call earlier was probably just a prank call. Maybe there is no connection."

"Prank call my foot. It's that Dallas Devil, I bet! Sounds like the caller is IN CLEVELAND! Maybe it was him in the Diner. It is only a thirty-minute drive from the Diner to your house! Lock your doors! I'm on my way over there now. "

Levenia picked up the phone, "What happened? Zita just flew out the door. Dallas Devil? Hunter, what is going on?"

"Levenia, I promise to catch you up soon." said Hunter.

"Okay, hon, I look forward to it." she said and hung up the phone.

Zita must have flown down the road to arrive at his home fifteen minutes later a loud voice announced Zita's arrival. Hunter let her in. "You didn't need to rush over. I'm a big boy. I can take care of myself."

Zita slammed the door behind her and locked it. "Maybe so, but you don't know what that guy's up to." King ran in the room and started rubbing against Zita's leg.

"I know he's a loner. One on one, I think I have the edge. He may have a gun, but I'd bet I'm quicker on the draw." He patted his shoulder holster and then put both hands on his hips. "Look, Zita, I appreciate your concern, but it is likely that call wasn't from him. Lots of kids play pranks. Did it myself when I was a teenager. And the report was that a young guy was seen in the Diner. They wouldn't know anything about the Dallas Devil, but they think it's fun to scare the sheriff, right?"

She met his gaze as she bent over to pick up the kitten. "Wrong. This is too much of a coincidence." Hunter scratched his ear. "Okay, you've got my back. But I don't need your help."

She swallowed hard and didn't reply.

Hunter edged close enough to get a whiff of Zita's perfume as he reached to scratch King's head. Taking a deep breath, he advised her, "Don't get too close. I'll admit the guy's dangerous. Anyone who hurts kids doesn't have a conscience. So don't get in his way. You hear me?"

Zita rocked on her toes. "Okay, Boss; it's your call. But I'm able to take care of myself, too." She dropped back to her heels.

When the cell phone rang and "Unknown Caller" flashed across the screen, Hunter flinched, causing Zita to frown. This time when he answered the phone, the voice was husky. He turned on the speaker phone so Zita could listen. "You're scared, aren't you? Calling in your fe-male deputy to help. Not smart," his guffaw interrupted. "Well, you're too quick. Sweat a little. Today's not the day I'm coming after you, Sher-iff." Click.

Zita asked, "Do you believe him? Saying today's not the day may be just to throw you off-guard."

"I know that. I do think he wants to taunt me before acting."

"It's more like before *attacking*." She moistened her lips. "Hunter, don't you think we should seek some help? The guy's crossed state lines. Couldn't we call in the FBI?"

Holding up both palms, Hunter said, "No, I aim to handle this myself."

He gripped her shoulder. "Please, Zita, go home. Today was supposed to be your day off. I'll call you if I need you."

Zita squeezed his hand. "Alright, I'll go; I don't like this one bit. But you're the boss." She put King down on the floor.

She didn't have to tell him to make sure he locked the door behind her. He used a key and also secured a chain in place, even though he knew that provided little protection. It would give him a few extra moments to ward off an intruder.

53

# Chapter 5

After the long weekend, Shannon called Hunter to let him know the final paperwork was cleared and the memorial site on the Tollar Plantation was chosen. "I've talked to the minister at the Zion church about a graveside service for Goldie, and I wanted to run a few things by you," she said.

The memorial service provided the diversion he needed, even though it moved his focus to another morbid subject, a sixty-year-old overdue funeral. Hunter shifted gears in his brain to focus on Shannon's call. Her next statement threw him sideways. "Before I start discussing the funeral, I have a question. What in the world are all those bottles on tree limbs or sticks in front yards? I see them in everyone's yard."

"Ha, ha, ha. You're in Mississippi. It's another superstition hung over from Africa. They're called Bottle Trees. You want to know the history?"

"Sure, tell it all. I'm interested in cultures and I love people who are curious."

Not sure how to respond, Hunter still saw it as a reprieve from chaos, confusion, and fear. He was glad he sought out information about the oddity. He could relay it to a newcomer to the area.

"Bottle trees were first used to decorate gravesites. Cedar trees were often near graves. If a tree limb hung over a grave, relatives, or maybe friends, stuck multi-colored bottles on the limbs. Perhaps this was like putting flowers on a grave, except bottles don't wilt. Then they put them in front of houses expecting to protect the occupants. They believe these trees have powers, especially the blue bottles. Wind blows through the necks of the bottles and chases evil spirits away. If homes don't have trees with limbs in the right places, they substitute wooden poles and place bottles on them. Sometimes they put dirt from a grave in those bottles."

"Amazing!" said Shannon. "I noticed all the bottle trees around your apartment."

"Yes, V is back in town. He clearly loves the bottle trees. When I saw a lemon-colored Rolls Royce drive in downstairs Sunday, I knew it had to be V. He came up to let me know he was back the other day. Said he had all the bottle trees installed to keep his place safe while he was out of town. Since I am here, he is going to keep them up. It's another world in the Delta." said Hunter.

Shannon sighed. "Well, I guess I'm a long way from my roots too. Bottle trees, ghosts dressed in red, and mojo stones aren't in my realm. But I won't knock them. Let people have their superstitions. Maybe someday I'll discover I have some of my own. You know what Hunter? After I saw V's guitar and how much Goldie influenced the music industry, I asked myself why not establish a museum for my grandfather and the blues? I have so much land out at my place and it can be good for the local economy. Help everyone out here. Oh, and V approved the sale of the statue and is going to bronze it himself. It should be ready by the time we have the memorial service, but I have to give him a date."

She took a deep breath. "Now, back to the reason for my call. When I started this, I had no idea a memorial service for

Goldie Parsons would be such a big deal. Somehow the national media has gotten wind of it and they're going to be here. Plus, there are several Goldie Parsons' Fan Clubs around the country and their members are ready to attend. It has spread out of control."

Hunter sat at his table, pulled out a calendar, and made a couple of notes. "When are you thinking of having the ceremony?"

"Let's make it quick, so it won't give outsiders a lot of time to plan. I was thinking about the second Saturday in December. The preacher's available then and maybe the cold weather will thin out the crowd. As you know, since you said you were there when they picked up Goldie's remains, I had the bones cremated, so it'll just be an urn to bury. I had my mother and grandmother's remains dug up from Magnolia Cemetery in Mobile and cremated as well. They will all be buried together, and we will have a slab poured on top of the site to keep things from disappearing. We've had enough of that in my family. I had to pay an exorbitant amount, but I got the tombstone engraved with the names and dates and it'll be in place. All will be held at the gravesite. I've selected some Bible quotes for the preacher from Mount Zion Church to read."

She nodded. "One thing's in order, though, a rendition of his two songs by a famous black singer. From all I've heard, Goldie and El would like that." She gulped. "So would I."

"Have you thought about Boo Radney? I heard he moved back here when he semi-retired--he still does gigs from time to time. So he might be available. Got a powerful voice."

"Sounds great. I'll check with him. The entire ceremony shouldn't take more than an hour."

"Don't count on it. You're going to get people who want to speak, even if they never knew Goldie. He's a legend. And what about afterwards? The media will expect a reception."

"Oh, hell! You mean I have to feed them to come annoy me? Why does it have to be so complicated? Next, you'll say Goldie should lie in state for a day or two. Ha, glad that can't happen since there's not a body to view." She took a deep breath. "Let me see what else I have to do to line things up. I don't want any glitches."

"Keep me posted, please. I'll need to call in the troops." He chuckled.

Shannon made a smacking sound. "Thanks, Hunter. You've been such a big help. I threw you a kiss. Call you tomorrow."

The rest of the day was quiet, but he paid attention to his surroundings everywhere he went. Hunter glanced towards his cell phone, expecting another call from the Devil, but nothing came. Zita was also out of the office, following up on another case, and Chan was out sick, leaving Hunter mostly alone for much of the day to catch up on paperwork and make a plan for Shannon's event.

When his day was done, he walked back to his apartment, checking for anything unusual as he made his way down the sidewalk. He wasn't going to hide. When he unlocked the front door, King strutted past his feet without stopping. He looked at the kitten and said, "Go ahead and ignore me. I've got too many things on my mind to talk to you anyhow. Besides, you wouldn't be of any help." He picked up King's Bowl and refilled it with fresh water. "All you care about is eating and sleeping, but you did one good deed at my party the other day; you scared the devil out of Carlton, ha, ha. Now remember how to do that if the

Dallas Devil comes snooping around." He leaned over close as he could get to the kitten's ear and whispered, "You hear me?"

With a hearty hiss, King ran past him into the bedroom and crawled under the bed, still making loud noises. Poking his head out for one more hiss, he retreated back under the bed. A light snoring soon signaled that King was sound asleep.

After fixing himself a steak and two baked potatoes Hunter headed to bed, the next day was to be an early one.

His cell phone rang, causing Hunter to immediately wake up and check the screen. It was one a.m. "Unknown Caller" flashed across the screen. He grumbled into it, "Hello."

"Good morning, Sheriff," a gruff voice replied. "Know who this is?"

"Yeah, I know who the hell you are. The psychopath who preys on young kids. Why are you here? Dallas too hot for you?"

"No, I've still got the police befuddled. Callie Fogg's murder was never solved. Does that bug you? As for me, kids are exciting to entice, but I'm becoming bored. I need new prey and I think you will do well. Your second story apartment isn't the best place to hide from your troubles. You could fall out the window and fires start in the most unusual places. You should be concerned that I'm outside looking up at your window. You have a good view, though. All those bottle trees sparkle in the moonlight."

Hunter made a fist. It angered him to be reminded of another unresolved case. It also made him determined to find out how much this creep knew about it. Keeping the lights off in his room, Hunter eased out of bed to the floor, with King jumping out of the way. He went into his bathroom, balanced on the edges of the tub and stared out of the small window above the shower.

In the dim streetlight just outside V's front door downstairs, Hunter saw a figure outlined in the dim light from the neighbor's front porch but could not distinguish any features. *I've got to keep him on the line till I can get down there.*

He put his phone on speaker, climbed down, and jerked on a pair of pants piled on his bedroom floor. He grabbed his gun and eased his way to the front door and the stairs, since the figure he saw was in the back. Hunter took a quick glance out the living room window and could still see the person outlined in the darkness.

"What do you want? Let's meet and talk about this like men." He tried to control his breathing so the caller wouldn't know he was on the move.

"No fun in meeting. Boring. Besides, you were out to get me in Dallas; you failed, it's my turn." His voice became higher pitched when he added. "Aha! I saw your door open. You're already on your way down here. Don't bother. I'll be long gone before you get downstairs. But I'll be back!"

Click.

When Hunter picked up pace and raced around the corner, the motion detector light clicked on, blinding him as he tried to look up and down the street. He ran to where the figure stood only moments before, but no one was in sight. He slammed a fist into his other hand. "Damn it to Hell! I thought I had him this time."

He sat on the bottom step of the stairs, rested his forehead into his hand and debated what to do. He might try to chase the culprit himself, but he needed help. He dialed Zita. He gave her a rundown on what happened and told her, "Get on the street a few blocks past my house. He may have a car we haven't seen before. I'm going to drive around my house to see if I can spot anything." He told her different areas to cover. "Look, I know this is an exercise in futility, but maybe we'll get lucky. Report back to me if you see anything, anything at all."

Spotting a light inside indicating V was now home, Hunter walked over to his front door to warn him but was greeted with, "Hello, Sheriff," from the dark entryway.

"Hi V, sorry it's so late, but I need to tell you…"

"No worries, my man." V said. The next sound was the sharp click of a gun trigger being released. "I got your back. The mojo let me know something was up. The little man stood across the street for about a minute, then he scooted into the dark as soon as you came out."

"Thanks, I will drive around the house to be sure all is safe."

"No problem." V patted his pistol. "If there is, we can deal with it."

"Thanks." Hunter walked towards his car, determined not to waste time.

Hunter drove down each street at fifteen miles an hour and paused to glance into doorways or other recessed places. Zita did the same in other parts of town. Thirty minutes later, they ended up at the Crossroads, the last place this crazy person might be. Except for one man, Zita spotted sleeping outside an abandoned warehouse, they found nothing. Hunter told her, "Thanks for coming. Go home and go back to bed. We'll hash this over in the morning."

Hunter took his own advice, but he didn't get a moment's sleep; he tossed and turned, his mind staying active until his alarm sounded at six a.m.

For King, it was as if nothing happened last night. The cat stood by his feeding dish and meowed, then he moved away. Hunter refilled the food and water dishes, saying, "At least you could give me a little sympathy, but you're just a damn cat and you don't care." King ate his food and lapped at his water, never looking up.

Trying to clear the fog in his head, Hunter made coffee and popped a bagel into his toaster. As he sat there eating the buttered morsel, it gnawed at him that the Dallas Devil was so brazen last night. But how far would he go? The man seemed to be hanging around Cleveland, ready to taunt him at every opportunity.

He finished his breakfast and went to the bathroom to shave, all the while mulling over where to look and who to put on the case. One person who wouldn't be assigned was Carlton. He would make sure that guy didn't even answer the phone.

Ideas raced through his brain. He had to find this guy before he, or someone else, got hurt. Shannon's children came to mind. Had the criminal seen them come to his house? Would he target them?

Hunter finished dressing, added his shoulder holster and gun, and took the elevator downstairs. This was going to be a very long day.

# Chapter 6

Feeling a distinct chill in the air and seeing streets dusty from the empty cotton fields, resulted in Hunter's decision to drive to the office that morning. He also had to bring King with him to the office. V was fixing water lines in his own kitchen, directly under Hunter's kitchen, and needed free access to the apartment. Concerned King would bother the repairman, he put him in his crate and brought him to the office.

As King snoozed quietly under Hunter's desk, He texted Zita to take her time coming in due to their late night. He sipped his coffee and was checking his emails when the squeal of wheels turning the corner caused him to look up. It was Shannon's red Jeep.

She slammed her car to a stop in the middle of the street, she hopped out and ran to the office door, flinging it open. Charles, dressed in Lone Ranger pajamas, was a step behind. Shannon burst inside and yelled, "She's missing. She wasn't in her bed this morning. Do something, Hunter!"

Hunter didn't have to ask who was missing. He knew it was Karla. Had his premonition, his fear come true? He started to speak, but couldn't get a word in. He was surprised to see this level-headed woman in such a panic.

She walked the office lobby in a circle as she rattled on. "Oh, my God. Here I took my father's children by that damn trophy wife of his. You know they are my little half-brother and half-sister, right? She abandoned them. I thought I could take care of them. I gave up my job and moved to Mississippi to provide a life for us. Now I've lost Karla. I think Frederica took her."

Charles went to face Hunter. "Where's my sister? She can't take care of herself. If Mama has her, she won't take care of her." His eyes clouded over. "Why didn't she take me too? Karla needs me!" He turned and slapped Shannon's arm. "Why didn't you stop her? Karla doesn't understand. You were supposed to protect us from her." He sank into a chair sobbing. Hunter's heart broke to see him so distraught.

Realizing she needed to calm down for his sake, Shannon stooped and put her arm around him. "We'll find them; don't cry, Charles."

Hunter helped calm down Shannon, and then he took charge. "We'll find her, but where do I start looking? Can you tell me everything that happened? When was the last time you saw her? What was she wearing? Did you hear anything unusual?"

In a shaky voice, Shannon replied, "I got her and Charles to bed last night at about nine since school is still out. The old house is so big they each have a room of their own on the second floor. She had on pajamas with pink bunnies...oh, Good Lord, please let her be safe. I'm a sound sleeper and I didn't hear any noise from those old stairs."

Charles then said, "I heard a noise by the window in my room. I got up and looked outside but didn't see anything. I think it was almost midnight. I was too sleepy to see the clock right. I checked on Karla and she was in her room in bed."

"Are you sure?" Hunter asked. "Or did you just see covers bunched up?

Charles shook his head fast. "I pulled down the covers. She was there then. It was still dark, so I went back to bed." He sniffled. "Please find her."

Hunter patted Charles' shoulder. "We will, Son, don't worry; Karla will be safe." *I hope I'm telling the truth. Who in the world has her?*

Hunter looked into the blue eyes of a pale-faced Shannon. "What time did you discover she was missing?"

"When I got up, about an hour ago?"

Where did you look, inside, outside, around the river or the cotton bin?"

She took a deep breath, released Charles, and stood. "I went to call them for breakfast. Let's see, first, only Charles came down to eat. Then we both knew something was wrong. I ran to Karla's room, and then to Charles'. She slips in there and sleeps in his bed sometimes if he's gone. Then I checked the other rooms upstairs. Next, we searched every room in the house, even the closets. We kept calling her name, but she didn't respond." Her lips quivered and her voice shook. "When we went outside and she wasn't in the yard, worry consumed me, but I didn't call you because I thought I should look down the street and by the old Oak tree, they like to play there, in case she wandered off. Oh, God. She wasn't anywhere. So, we got in my car and came here." She shoved a pointed finger into Hunter's chest. "We need to find her. Help me!" Panic laced with anger was in her voice.

"Try to calm down, Shannon." He pulled up a chair. "You and Charles wait here. Let me call Zita and we'll go out looking." He pointed to his percolator. "Get some coffee and I will send Deputy Chan to get something to eat for Charles. I think there's a few doughnuts in a box on the table. Help yourselves. I'll keep you posted. Chan, can you also start writing up this report?"

Hunter made a quick call to Zita and she replied, "I'm on it right now." He gave his deputy instructions on which area to search.

Hopping up, Chan nodded. He directed Shannon and Charles to his office. Carlton had wandered in the office and was sent to get something to eat for Charles. Hunter left the office and headed for his own patrol car. The search was on.

Zita was already dressed and heading out the door when Hunter called. A few sips of orange juice was all she managed. On her way, she recalled a conversation with Levenia about Shannon's children. She'd heard they were deserted by their mother and although Zita felt a strange tension when she was around Shannon, little Karla touched her heart. So did Charles' concern for his sibling. They had a bond that was admirable for kids so young.

Mind awhirl, Zita wondered how serious this situation was. Then unexpected goose bumps popped out on her arms as the Dallas Devil came to mind. It was equally as likely that he was responsible for this. Is this where he went last night after leaving Hunter's place?

She remembered from studying about mental illness in college that psychopaths have no conscience and no compunction about acting in a violent way. If revenge was their goal, they took action to achieve it any way they could.

Nonetheless, as she drove away from her house, her Catholic roots surfaced. Making a Sign of the Cross, she prayed, "Let Karla be okay, Lord, and I promise to say the rosary every day for a week." She crossed her fingers, then uncrossed them. "I'll even try to understand Shannon, maybe become her friend." Her optimistic nature returned and hope lifted her spirits.

Wracking her brain, she tried to put herself in the little girl's shoes. What if it was her mother who took her? Where would they have gone? Zita drove up and down several streets. When she didn't see Karla right away, her heart sank. Unsure of what to do next, she remembered a group of swings in the Elementary school play yard. She thought, *Maybe, just maybe...*

Her heart skipped a beat when she spotted a child there this early in the morning. She thought it was a little girl from the color of the pajamas, but she was too far away to identify her. She pulled up to the curb and dashed over to the swing set. "Karla," she called out as she approached, right hand resting on her gun, "is that you?"

The child turned to see Zita. When Karla recognized her, she hopped off the swing, and ran toward Zita. "Oh, Karla, how did you get here?" Zita asked as the child wrapped her arms around the deputy's legs.

Karla sucked in her bottom lip. "A man brought me, but he left," she sobbed.

Zita looked all around. Nobody was in sight. "A man? Not your mother? How long ago was that Honey?"

With a shrug, Karla said, "I don't know who it was. It wasn't my mom; it was a man. He came into my bedroom, he wore a black hood, and said if I didn't go with him, he'd hurt Charles and Shannon. I didn't want that to happen. I was scared. We drove around a lot and then he let me out here, and he went away."

*He takes her and drops her off, nothing else? She looks okay, no wounds or signs of assault. What is going on here? It definitely isn't her mother, then.* Zita was baffled.

Zita remembered that the old home they lived in was in the middle of being restored. Maybe it still had a couple of windows with broken glass? He must have gotten in that way. "Which way did he go?"

Karla pointed left. "I saw him stop and turn that way." She pointed to her right. Then he disappeared." She shrugged. "That's all." When Zita looked she didn't see anyone at all. She took Karla to the car and put her into the front passenger seat. "I've got to call your Mommy, er, Shannon, and the sheriff and let them know you're alright. You are all right, aren't you?" Karla's pajamas were intact, so Zita felt relief when Karla nodded agreement.

When Zita updated Hunter, he said, "Wow! I'm sure glad she's okay. My gut tells me it was that monster who took her. He's doing anything he can to torment me," Hunter radioed Zita who was heading back to the office with Karla. She smiled at the child who had fallen asleep in the passenger seat.

Hunter continued, "I'll let Shannon know she's safe, but don't say anything about the Devil. We need to get her checked, too. I will call the doctor. Bring her to the station and let's see what she can tell us. I don't expect too much." He hung up.

*     *     *

Charles spoke up at the reunion in the sheriff's office. After the doctor reported she was in good health, he ignored the adults' plea to back off and lit into his sister after she told him what happened. "You know better than to go off with a stranger, I don't care what he told you." He slapped her bottom hard.

Karla sniffled. "I didn't want to go off with him. He dragged me out of bed, and he said he was going to hurt you and Shannon if I didn't go with him."

When Charles raised his hand again, Hunter grabbed it. "Stop it." He dragged the boy to a chair and plopped him into it. "Stay here and don't say another word. We need to talk to Karla."

Wide-eyed, the boy slinked down mumbling, "Go ahead and tell them what you know, Karla." Poking out his bottom lip, he complied to Hunter's order and kept silent.

Hunter and Zita left Shannon with Charles, took Karla into Zita's office, and closed the door. Hunter sat in her office chair while Zita gave Karla a cold RC Cola from her small fridge and guided Karla to an old wooden chair. He asked, "Sweetie, can you guess how old the man was?"

Karla looked up at Hunter and took a sip of her soda. " I think he was about as old as my mother."

*Huh, so he is much younger than I suspected.* "What color shirt was he wearing?"

She pointed to Hunter's khaki shirt. "That color."

Hunter asked, "Do you know what color pants he wore?"

Karla's head bobbed. "Dark. Oh, he had on a cap and his shirt had some numbers on it, but I don't know what they were." She shrugged again. "That's all I know." Hunter saw confusion cross Zita's face. Karla had told her the man wore a black hood.

Zita stooped down beside her. "Honey, was the number on his shirt, or on a badge like mine?" She tapped her own badge.

"Yeah," Karla replied. "Like yours."

"How tall was he? Was he fat or skinny?"

She hesitated. "Skinny, maybe, and he was lots taller than me." She patted her tummy. "I'm hungry."

"Thanks, honey. That's enough for now. We'll let you go with your mom, er, Shannon." Zita escorted the child back to Shannon and told her it was okay to leave. Deputy Chan followed them home to sweep the house in case of another break in. Zita and Hunter were to inspect the crime scene later on in the morning.

Zita returned to Hunter, hands on her hips, she asked, "What do you make of all this? That little girl is usually very quiet; her brother speaks for her. Now, she's speaking up loud andclear."

Scratching his chin, Hunter squinted. "She kept glancing at that photo of Rich in his uniform, the one on the wall. And she focused on me too. Made me think she was describing both of us."

"You think that little kid is making this up? Kids often do that to please us. Hell, adults do too, sometimes."

"I don't think anything yet. Just speculating because of the khaki uniform shirt and the badge with numbers on it." He cleared his throat. "But nothing is conclusive. Now, let's go check Shannon's house and see if we can get an idea of who broke in"

"Well, I can guess." said Zita as she went back to her office.

*     *     *

Hunter wanted to drive out to the Tollar Plantation by himself, but Zita wouldn't have it. "What if that crazy killer follows you out there? Then Shannon and the kids only have you to protect them? No, two of us is better than one," she insisted.

He couldn't argue with her logic. He didn't mention that the forensics team, which consisted of two officers who also ticketed speeders, was to come out to the house soon.

When Hunter and Zita arrived, improvements to the old Tollar Plantation house were obvious. Zita whistled, "Will you look at that place? It is beautiful, well, it will be when she is done." Shannon had replaced the roof and scaffolding was set up in various locations around the house; workers were replacing boards and preparing to paint the exterior of the entire house. It was clear Shannon was trying to return the place to its original charm.

Hunter and Zita walked up the porch steps and across the wrap-around porch to the old screen door. The original door was salvaged, and the screen door had its old mesh replaced with new. Hunter grinned at the novelty of turning the knob on the old-fashioned doorbell and Shannon answered the door.

Before she let them in, Shannon said, "Look, don't put too much faith in Karla's statement. I think she felt like she had to give you answers even though they were not true. She even asked me if she could go to jail for lying to the cops. I told her to calm down and take a nap. She's asleep on the sofa," she cautioned. "She was tired out, so I hope you don't need to talk to her again."

"No, we just want to take a look around," Hunter assured her. "Have you noticed anything suspicious? Any evidence that someone was messing around? What about the people working on the house?"

"I hate to admit to being so careless, but I haven't gotten a few windows fixed yet. The worst one is the broken window in the kitchen. It wouldn't be too hard to get in there. Oh, another thing, I'm not sure because I was in such a hurry to leave to hunt for Karla, but the front door may have been left open when I rushed out this morning."

Hunter stepped inside. "You mind if we check the kitchen first?"

Leading them into the kitchen, Shannon pointed out the broken window by the dining table. Hunter looked outside and spotted glass on the ground and a pile of window screens propped up against the house. "Do you know if the screen was up before the window was broken, Shannon?"

"I'm not sure. They are painting the house, so the painters might have taken it off."

Zita heard a knock on Shannon's front door and went to check. When she came back into the kitchen, she tapped Hunter on the shoulder. "The forensics team is outside; I will tell them to check this window and look for other possible places to enter the house."

"Tell them to watch where they step. It sprinkled again yesterday, so it's a little muddy out there. Maybe they'll find fresh footprints."

Hunter turned to Shannon and asked, "Where's Karla's room?"

Everyone walked to the grand staircase in the center of the house. "Up there," Shannon said "Go down the hallway to the second door on the left. I'll stay down here."

At first Hunter wondered where Charles was since he was not with Shannon, but he soon found out at the top of the stairs when he came tearing out of his room with fingers in the shape of a gun and a badge made of cardboard stuck to his T-shirt with tape. "Don't come any closer, or I'll shoot," he blared out. Laughing, he said, "Scared ya, didn't I, Sheriff?"

Hunter grinned; glad to see the young boy finally acting like the child he was, the sheriff played along. He held up both hands. "Don't shoot; I wouldn't want to have to shoot back." He lowered his hands. "Do you mind showing me your sister's room?" He walked down the long hallway and opened the closest door. "This it?"

Charles nodded. "I didn't touch anything. Shannon said not to." He stood in the doorway as Hunter entered the room and looked around.

He noticed the pink bedspread was rumpled and left unmade, covers shoved aside. A pillow was indented the shape of a small child's head. A pair of tiny slippers were under a chair. Hunter mused over that as he looked at them. Normally, a child would put them on, or find a pair of shoes to wear to go outside. He went to the bed and lifted the edge of the cover touching the floor.

"Whoa!" Hunter exclaimed. He picked up a candy wrapper, sniffing it to see if it was fresh. It was. Charles sneaked up behind him and asked, "What did you find?"

Regaining composure, he turned to the boy. "A candy wrapper. Do you know anything about it? Did she keep candy in her room?"

Charles shook his head. "Shannon doesn't let us have candy in our rooms and I know we didn't have any last night." Charles asked as he looked at the wrapper in Hunter's hand, "Where'd that come from?"

As he bagged the wrapper and stuck it in his pocket, a hint of a memory of a Snickers' wrapper in a past case whirled around in Hunter's mind. He couldn't pinpoint it, so he stopped letting it nag at him and forced it out of his thoughts.

Charles accompanied Hunter as he headed downstairs. The boy was unusually chatty, but Hunter let him rant on.

Hunter walked outside to check in with Zita and the forensic team inspecting the property. He was greeted at the front porch by a deputy who stood holding up a plastic bag. Inside was a cigarette. "We found this by a couple of footprints under the window. Take a close look, Sheriff."

Hunter took the bag and looked closer at its contents. "What the Hell! Looks like lipstick on the filter. We'll have to ask Shannon if she noticed anyone painting the house wearing red lipstick. If so, they were a bit careless to smoke this close to the house. If it didn't belong to a painter, maybe it was the kidnapper's. And criminals aren't always bright."

The deputy also told Hunter, "You were right about the footprints. We found boot marks, looks like they're from leather soles, but they are a small size. Too fresh to belong to anyone working outside before yesterday."

"Really?"

Hunter turned and called out to Shannon who just stepped out on the porch, "Shannon," he asked, "Do you smoke? Do you know anyone else around here who does?"

Shannon replied, "No, I quit years ago."

Hunter held up the cigarette and Shannon gave a half laugh. "Not my shade of lipstick but my, er, cleaning lady wears lipstick. Might be hers. Where'd you find it?"

"Next to the kitchen window. Why would she be smoking there? Does she have small feet?"

"She always went outside to smoke. She was here yesterday afternoon cleaning the windows. Those painters can make a mess! Maybe she saw something while she was working. I never checked her shoe size."

Hunter didn't say anything, but his brain kept spinning. *Anything is possible.*

"Can I have her contact information?" He put the information on his phone for his next stop and directed Zita to ride back to the office with the forensics team when they left. They didn't really find anything conclusive. She didn't like the idea of him going off alone, but she was needed back in the office. No telling what would happen if Carlton was left alone too long.

He told Charles and Karla, who just got up from her nap, "You kids just do whatever Shannon tells you, okay? Everything's going to be alright."

Karla nodded, but Charles stared at the ceiling. As Hunter left in his car, he heard Charles mumble, "You better be sure it is."

Hunter drove back to the main road, turned left onto Hwy 8 and went to an old farm subdivision located about a mile down the road. The Delta was spotted with these sort of neighborhoods. The homes were originally built in the 1950s and sold to black farmhands. Unfortunately, the farm was sold, but the black homeowners, who worked hard to own their land, were determined to remain.

It was almost December, and a chill surged through his body. He almost missed the address Shannon gave him, a modified row house, larger than other homes in the neighborhood. He pulled to a stop in front of the house which was in need of a paint job.

When he first stepped on the porch, he rested his hand on his gun, but he need not have worried. After ringing the bell, a neatly dressed woman came to the door and a whiff of lavender greeted his nose. The lady was short in stature so he could see over her inside the home, and it was spotless. Much to his surprise, she welcomed him inside and they sat at her dining room table. It was set with real crystal and sterling silver, a Wallace pattern much like his own he'd inherited from his mother. His eyes widened at seeing Haviland china plates in the Vareene pattern that he boxed up and saved from his mother's collection. Also, crystal water goblets and linen napkins graced the table to give everything an elegant finishing touch.

"Shannon told me all about the Goldie Parson's case and how you solved it, quite a story!" said Jacashia Smith as she poured Hunter a cup of coffee.

"Thank you, ma'am. Your home is beautiful." said Hunter as he took a sip.

"I can tell my home surprises you, Sheriff. Sometimes it surprises me, too. The house belonged to my parents and I inherited it." She adjusted the flatware at one place setting. "You see, I worked at a jewelry store in Jackson and I wanted some nice things, so I took my pay in trade."

She looked at him sideways and he noticed crowsfeet in the corner of her eyes. *She's not as young as I first thought. Maybe in her late forties. But not so old that she couldn't get through the window. No, Karla said it was a man, but who knows?*

"Can you understand that Sheriff?"

"What?" He refocused. "Oh, sure. Everyone wants some nice things." He asked her a few questions about lipstick, where she was that morning, and if she owned any work boots.

"Of course I do. I work in the yard quite a bit. I have a beautiful rose garden behind the fence, but I will tell you, it is hard getting good shoes. I am not that tall, but my feet are large for my size, I wear a size ten ladies."

Hunter remembered the forensic team working at Shannon's place said the print was small and size ten was not small. Also, Hunter observed the lipstick Jacashia was wearing. It was a much darker shade than the color on the cigarette tip Hunter was convinced she wasn't guilty of taking Karla away. So he thanked her for her time and left, still a bit in awe of the finery in that shack. But it did prove to him that if you want something bad enough to sacrifice to get it, you can achieve your goal.

He turned onto Hwy 8 again to head back to the office, and his thoughts switched to his own home and furnishings. If he had delicate crystal like Jacashia's, would King hop on the table, swish his tail, and break each goblet into a hundred pieces? He chuckled at his own admission. *Not likely. Cats are graceful.*

He slapped the side of his head. *Good grief! King's been in that carrier all morning. No litter box access. Damn! I bet it stinks to high heaven.*

He flung open the door to the office and headed for King's cage. When he looked behind his desk, the cage was empty, but clean.

Chan ambled in with the cat in his arms and a wide grin on his face. "Took him outside to do his business. I've had a cat, so I'm surprised, but glad, that he did it outside. I didn't see a litter box around anywhere."

"Thanks. I intended to take him home earlier. Then we got tied up with this case."

Easing King back into his carrier, Chan shut the door. "That cat's smart. Seems to know who to avoid. Ha, when Carlton walked into the hall, he arched his back."

"Not too smart. Hell, he does the same thing to me and I'm the one who feeds him."

A loud "Meow" reinforced Hunter's statement. "See what I mean?" He picked up the carrier and headed out the door. "I'm taking you home and I'll get some lunch."

Hunter turned to Chan. "Hold things down till I get back. Call me if you need me. Better yet, call King."

*　　*　　*

At home, repairs done, Hunter released King and let him roam around the loft while he fixed himself a ham sandwich and poured a glass of milk. When a tiny rock fell off the sole of one of his boots, before he could pick it up, King rushed to sniff it and play with it. But when Hunter reached down to retrieve the rock, King scratched the top of his hand.

"Quit that, damn you!" Hunter slapped at the cat, but he scooted out of reach. Wetting a paper towel, Hunter dabbed at the small amount of blood from the wound, drying it off. Then he got a Band-Aid and covered it.

Hunter picked up the rock and held it up to his nose. He knew enough about cats to know only something smelly or shiny would interest them. It was caked with mud, but it definitely smelled like chocolate, maybe it was a piece of the candy bar.

Despite efforts to force unwanted thoughts from his mind, all he could think of was the mojo stone. But that stone was much larger. Where did he step on the chocolate? It had to get on his boot at Shannon's house. He scratched his head.

Then he looked at King perched on the headrest of his lounge chair. "Too bad you're not a dog. Then I could sic you on this case and you could make yourself useful!" He got a plastic bag from his kitchen cabinet, put the hard, dried up piece of candy inside, and stuck the baggie in his pocket. "King let's not tell anyone about this. I'm keeping it as a clue, just in case something crazy comes up and ties it to the case."

For the first time, King came over and rubbed his body against Hunter's pants' leg in a nuzzling fashion. When his master reached down and patted his head, the cat didn't run off. A smile crossed the sheriff's face, developing into a broad grin when King jumped up into his arms. A pact was made.

# Chapter 7

Hunter spent the morning at the department store, picking out the right size collar and harness for King. An active cat, King started trying to run out the front door when Hunter left for work in the morning. He did so well in the office, Hunter decided it was time to try and train him to walk on a leash. As he stared at the small harnesses for small dogs, he wondered, *When did I get to the point that I am actually going to walk my cat to the office?*

Since King made friends with Hunter, he was concerned about leaving him at home alone. The Dallas Devil knew where he lived and it was known that most serial killers had no compunction about hurting animals. He couldn't do this every day, but it wouldn't hurt to see if King was able to walk on a leash. Hunter didn't want to have a litter box in the office, so a leash was essential. *If he gets too comfortable, that damn cat will take over my office just like he did my house.*

When he entered the building, he walked the harnessed King into his office and shut the door. Zita, who also just came in, said, "Harley, I was just coming to get you. Shannon got a phone call from the kids' mother, Frederica, wanting money. Shannon didn't take it seriously since she wasn't the one who took Karla like she originally thought. She found a note taped to the door this morning. It said, 'I want the kids.' … Is that King in your office?"

"Yes, crazy isn't it? I put the harness on him, and he took right to it. Walked with me to the office like he has done it his whole life. Smart cat. About Shannon. she should know how to handle this."

"She's a lawyer, so I'm pretty sure she has legal custody. She says the woman's a drunk, probably on drugs–and nuts to boot."

"Okay," Hunter replied as he headed out the door. "Let's go back to her house to check out the note. Fredricka is from Mobile, right? I'll message the other officers to be on the lookout for Alabama plates. Maybe we can bring her to the office, ask her a few questions, and give her a bit of a scare. Maybe she will leave afterwards."

*     *     *

Hunter and Zita knew today was going to be one of those days as they drove down the driveway to the Tollar house and saw smoke pillowing in the air from a distance. Hunter slammed on the gas and raced past Shannon's house, the great oak tree, and the cotton bin and down the dirt road that led to the back field. He saw Shannon on the front porch of the house and noticed her confused expression as he zoomed past her front door. Hunter brought the car to a screeching stop at the source of the fire, a pile of wood in front of Mama Cheche's row house, the remains of the old porch.

Tippiny hired workmen to replace the destroyed porch before she left Cleveland. The house was vacant at the moment, but the power and water remained on. Shannon and Jacashia kept it clean and ready for Tippiny when she wanted to come home.

When Hunter spotted the large pile of wood aflame in the front yard just a few feet from the steps leading to the porch, he jumped out of his car and popped the trunk lid. Snatching a fire extinguisher from it, he put out the fire in a couple of minutes, saving the structure.

Shannon pulled up behind him in her red Jeep. She rushed past Hunter to the front door, unlocked it, and dashed inside the house to be sure it was safe. "Nobody here, and no fire inside," she called out panting. She flopped into one of the old chairs on the porch, relieved, "That crazy woman must have done this." *I'm not so sure,* thought Hunter, but he couldn't tell Shannon that.

"It's possible," said Hunter, which wasn't a lie.

Using a fallen limb, he poked through the foam-covered bits of wood, ash and dry newspaper. The newspaper showed the fire was intentionally set. He pulled out bits of the paper that remained. He couldn't tell the date, but *Mobile Press Register* was clear across the piece he held in his hand. He called over to Zita to show her what he found. She pulled an evidence bag out of her pocket and sealed the fragment in it.

Hunter walked over to where Shannon sat in one of the front porch rockers and said, "It's crazy. Makes no sense for anyone to start a fire in front of this house unless it was Fredrika then the newspaper fragment confirms it. Looks like her goal was to distract or upset you, Shannon." He then sat in an old chair next to Shannon.

"What are you thinking, Shannon? Is this a warning from the kid's mother?" Hunter asked as she handed him the note left on her door. He noticed Zita staying close by to hear what they were talking about, but not enough to be in the conversation. When he flipped the paper over, the words, "Want the kids" were written in almost illegible handwriting. He didn't have an example of the Devil's handwriting on him, but the one on this note looked familiar.

"I don't know. You see that note. It means she is here in Cleveland. I didn't expect her to drive out here from Alabama. I don't know what to think, Hunter." She sucked in the corner of her cheek. "I have legal custody, and I don't want Frederica coming here upsetting the kids. She's crazy and under the influence of drugs and drink." She jerked her head backwards. "Could she have started the fire? I wouldn't put it past Frederica. She burned down the house my father bought for the family in Mobile to get the insurance money."

Hunter decided Shannon was probably right–that action could be attributed to Frederica. Hunter wondered if the Dallas Devil knew about Mama Cheche's house and Shannon's troubles with Frederica. He glanced around, wondering if he was watching them now. Hiding by the river, maybe? He had to know about the Goldie Parsons case.

"I'm not giving that bitch Charles and Karla. She isn't getting any money out of me either. She got plenty when she burned down the house and sold the lot." Shannon said. "I don't have time to deal with her. It took a lot of doing to rush this, but I have permission to bury Goldie and my mom and grandmother in that spot."

Shannon pointed to a beautiful patch of grass in the distance across from Mama Cheche's front porch. Hunter saw the pink flags marking the spot waving in the breeze. She continued, "I like the idea of a museum as a tourist attraction, but that will take a while."

As Hunter rose to leave, Shannon clued him in about the funeral. "On a better note, Tippiny's coming," she said, "and Boo Radney agreed to sing Goldie's songs at the gravesite. See that pile of dirt next to the markers on the hill? The double vault for the urn is in place, and grandmother's, umm, Eleanor's urn, is ready to be put in before they cover the plot. I didn't want to leave it exposed. Too many nuts out there. Oh, I meant to tell you that I found a poem Eleanor wrote on the back of the wedding photo, and I had it put on her tombstone next to Goldie's. Here it is." She was able to quote it from memory:

*Light of my life,*

*Love of it, too.*

*His song lived long after*

*His life on Earth's through.*

Her voice quivered when she said she'd had lots of calls from reporters trying to dig out details of the event. "I didn't tell them anything, but they already knew the place and the time. They figured it out from small town gossip, I guess." She sighed. "So they'll turn out in numbers. I've also had calls from a Parsons' Fan Club. They're coming with a busload. I've arranged for Levenia to serve food on the grounds. If I can, I'd like to keep them out of my home."

Hunter didn't warn her, but he'd have placed a big bet that one reporter would be there in full force…the ambitious, persistent female who pursued him and had been his nemesis all the way back to Dallas.

*     *     *

Saturday, a cold and dreary day, matched the mood for a funeral. Skies overcast gave way to intermittent rainfall.

The entire police force in Cleveland and Bolivar County was overwhelmed. Hunter had not seen a situation like this since he was back in Dallas. Highway 8 and the parking lot of the Zion Baptist Church, just across the street from the Tollar Plantation road was inundated with vans, trucks, and cars with out-of-state licenses. Church members sat in the parking lot with signs reading: *Parking $5.* The Goldie Parsons Fan Club bus, parked beside the church, had Goldie's face plastered on the sides with *Reelin' Feelin'* written across the windows.

Shannon had hired Levenia to cater the event. She rented a huge tent, normally used for weddings, and was serving her famous dishes at twenty dollars a pop. The place was packed with reporters, TV camera men and women, and Goldie fans. The eatery had standing room only and was the warmest and driest place they could wait for the services to start. Even the elderly and children braved the elements bearing umbrellas, stepping over mud puddles and dodging splashes from passing cars. Everyone trekked along the dirt road together with a couple of people being transported in wheelchairs and on walkers. This was an event that would go down in history, one they were determined not to miss. The media vied for position to record it all. Attendees huddled under Levenia's tent, providing an endless stream of customers waiting to cover the two p.m. Memorial Service for the long-lost and long-dead famous singer Goldie Parsons.

Hunter arrived with Zita, but not as early as his deputies who had strategically planned for crowd control. City police were in the mix. "Look at that," Hunter waved a finger toward a deputy pointing left and right issuing orders. "Carlton's put himself in charge."

Zita laughed. "Well, somebody's gotta do it. Zita laughed as Harley tried to get the hard-working deputy's attention. "Aw, Hunter, let him be. He can't do much harm, can he? He needs the glory."

Hunter waved her off. Then he pulled the car in the spot behind Mama Cheche's old house. "Okay, I'll let Carlton think he's in charge, but you and I will keep an eye on him." It was one p.m., almost an hour before the ceremony, and the entire area was packed, along with the street being blocked by guests. A few chairs had been placed facing the table bearing the urn and some people brought their own, but most of the attendees stood shifting from foot to foot.

Hunter pointed to a man with a long beard. "Who's that guy, Zita? I haven't seen him around before."

Zita chuckled. "You won't. Whiskers works dawn to dark in his store and gas station out on the highway. He and Levenia are the town's biggest gossips. I'm surprised he came today, but he's friends with lots of blues singers who stop by his store for coffee and to catch up on the news. Besides, Goldie's our most famous blues singer."

It didn't seem appropriate that Goldie's remains were encased in a simple urn with a forest green background, but it was decorated. His wedding photo covered one side, and the guitar sculpture and his two song titles filled up space on the other. Goldie was a legend, and he'd become one with a single record, an unprecedented achievement in the musical field.

Hunter looked at the tombstone with the bronzed guitar firmly secured on top of it. A disheveled looking man walked over to it, pulled out a white handkerchief and dusted it off. When he turned around, Hunter smiled. *That's V, my oddball landlord.* It looked like V was up late last night working on his art. Hunter had seen him like this before.

Hunter let his mind drift to Shannon's appraisal of V. "He's quite a character," she had said, "with all that frizzy white hair in a ponytail held in place with a green rubber band. His raspy voice makes him sound like a very old man. And that Van

Dyke beard makes him look older than he is, I bet. How old do you think he is?"

"Seventy?"

"Nope, he just turned sixty-three. He was at the store when I went to pick up the statue. We had a few drinks and he told me how impressed he was with you. V may act weird, but he is a magnificent artist and sculptor known all over the world, and he has a great sense of humor. He calls himself 'A black man who made it in a white man's world.' Ha, with that ebony skin, he could probably pass for white if he wanted to, but he doesn't."

She had added, "You know, V is an American treasure, internationally known, but I was shocked to find he lived in a little town like Cleveland, until I found out he was born here."

Hunter's eyes widening made her add, "Oh, no offense about Cleveland. But this is a small town. Anyway, I didn't realize how famous he is, either. Now, I can see why. He's an extremely talented artist."

Hunter studied the work of art. Judging by the scrap metal artistic guitar where he spotted a dented aluminum pan in the middle, and various trashed objects of different shapes and sizes, he had to agree. "He's a genius with his hands." He was also a genius with animals. V was at the ceremony now but was to return home after the service. Hunter would not make it home till late.

V was going to look after King while Hunter was working today. King was fond of playing in V's warehouse. When he went in there to find the kitten last week, he found V sketching on a large canvas, focused on his "subject." Harley was amazed as King sat on a stool and posed for V. "Hunter, King is a unique creature! I am enthralled!"

"Okay," said a confused Hunter, "He isn't bothering you? I can keep him at my place."

"Oh, no!" said V, "Let this glorious creature wander! I will keep an eye on him. What a treasure!"

"Okay. I'm at my place if you need me to get him," said Hunter and he slowly walked back to his apartment. When he got home from work the next day, a cat door appeared in the corner of one of the warehouse doors.

A voice interrupted his musings. "Hey, there's Tippiny, way over on the other side. Flew in from D.C. yesterday. She's going to stay for Christmas." Zita's announcement brought Hunter back to the present. They both waved, and Tippiny waved back. "Oh, I see Shannon, right behind her," Zita said. "She brought the two kids. I bet they've never been to a funeral before."

"They may have gone to their dad's funeral. But maybe not." Hunter replied as he surveyed the area looking for any sign of trouble, but all seemed normal. There was a buzz, but it didn't drown out the rendition of Goldie's two songs playing on speakers.

Promptly at two p.m., Mayor Willis stepped up in a black raincoat buttoned to the top. In a heavy southern drawl, he praised a man he'd never met in a long paragraph full of adjectives.

Next, Shannon stood at the lectern with a microphone in her hand, while cameras clicked incessantly. Her speech was brief. She acknowledged that she never knew her grandfather but she had done her research to learn as much as she could. She announced that she'd had his wife's remains, and her mother's, placed in the vault already. Her final words were, "Now, he and his love, Eleanor, and their beloved daughter are together again at last. This is a great day."

As soon as she stepped aside, allowing others a chance to say their piece, the minister approached. More photos were taken. In his elderly, raspy tone, he said, "Thank you all for coming to honor a great man, Cleveland's oldest and most famous legend," he raised his voice, "our one and only GOLDIE PARSONS."

No sooner were the words out of his mouth than a loud explosion caused all in the audience to turn to the area it came from behind them. Two more big bangs followed. A person wearing a black hoodie darted forward, snatched the urn from its stand, and stuffed it into a cloth bag. Before people realized what was happening, the perpetrator made way into the crowd and vanished.

"The urn! The URN!" the preacher yelled as loudly as his elderly voice permitted. "Somebody stop him!" He pointed in a direction opposite the one the thief took. Screaming people ran in all directions. Some stumbled and fell on top of each other. They scrambled to their feet and rushed out of the area.

Hunter realized the noise came from large, loud firecrackers. TV cameras rolled. After glancing to see exactly where the sounds came from, he kept his eyes on the action. The minute he saw the runner with the urn, he made every effort to follow, but the crowd blocked his path, so he rushed to his car, made his way through the field, finagled around in the narrow path between cars, and took off. Unlike his usual cursing response, this time, he mouthed a prayer: *That damn Devil! It has to be him, or is it Frederica? God help me catch whichever one it is.* Then he spoke into his lapel mic, clipped to the epaulet on his shoulder, and gave his staff orders. Chan was told to stay on the scene and interview onlookers.

As he drove down the streets with cars parked on both sides narrowing the route, his brain raced. Since the thief was nowhere in sight, Hunter suspected that the criminal left in a car on the main road. If he caught up with the criminal, he didn't want to do anything to cause the urn to be broken. Quite likely, that could be used as a threat. Or, it could happen accidentally. That made his own position vulnerable. *Dear God, what approach should I use?*

With no signs of the person, Hunter soon had to admit that he wasn't going to have to make any such decisions. He kept driving around and hoped the paramedics who passed him heading for the scene wouldn't have any wounded to treat.

After an hour, he determined it was a lost cause and he returned to the Tollar Plantation to face the press and the other deputies who'd also been on the prowl. He'd kept in touch with them by radio, so he knew they had no luck, either.

First, he sought out Chan, who was still on the scene. As soon as Chan saw his boss, he left the reporter he was questioning and hurried to Hunter's side. He held up a raggedy backpack. "Found this in the street. Take a sniff. I think the firecracker was in it. And I found remnants of the other two between the street and the gravesite." He got a plastic bag from his pocket and showed it to his boss.

Hunter nodded. "How about the reporters; did you find anyone who got pictures of the thief?"

"Not yet, and I talked to quite a few. Seems like they were all distracted by the noise and he got away."

"Just our luck," Hunter replied. "And it might be a *she* Chan. Shannon was having trouble with Charles and Karla's mother. Well, let's go face the music."

With Zita, Chan, and the mayor beside him and Carlton wedging in, Hunter held a press conference in front of their office in town and made a brief statement. "We know the sound came from firecrackers. What's left of them have been retrieved. We don't know who the perpetrator was, and we have no suspects." A male reporter from CBS asked if he thought it was more than one person and Hunter said, "We don't know yet."

Another reporter asked about injuries and Hunter said he thought a couple of people were transported to the hospital, but none were in critical condition; they just had scrapes and bruises.

A female called out, "Do you think this is connected to your case in Dallas when the wrong man was incarcerated and…"

Hunter held up his hand and glared at Jenny Stein. "As I've stated, we don't know anything yet. That's all the questions I will take. We'll keep you posted." He turned and left.

*       *       *

Hunter soon returned to the crime scene and parked at Mama Cheche's where Carlton met him. Shannon had moved Tippiny to a spare room in her house so she could rest from the long trip home. She opened up the old shack for the officers, turning on the heat so they could have a place to work.

Chin high, Carlton announced, "I stayed on the scene and kept people in order." He cocked his head. "Well, as best I could. People with kids got away quickly. The others went wild. They ran in all directions."

Hunter nodded. He'd passed some of those on his own search. All were going helter-skelter. With a nod, Carlton said, "After Chan interviewed the preacher and the bystanders and got their contact information, some people seemed frozen in their tracks, at a loss as to what to do. So, I instructed the deputies to tell them to disperse and go home. I was surprised a bit when they followed my orders. The whole area cleared in record time."

*His deputies? This guy's got a nerve. But why bother to correct him? I only saw a few stragglers the last time I passed the area, so that's good. I wonder where all those reporters went. The Hilton and the Shackem Up Inn couldn't hold everyone. If they spend the night, they'll have to sleep in their vehicles.*

As if reading his mind, Carlton said, "I checked at Shackem Up Inn and they turned away dozens of reporters. Some went to Jackson for the night, but you can bet they'll be back tomorrow, Sheriff. And they'll come and go until this is settled." He squared his shoulders. "But we're ready for them, aren't we?"

Hunter turned his back and looked at where Goldie should have been buried in the distance. *Ready for them? Hell, no! How can we be? We don't have a clue about what this criminal is up to. We don't even know who it is.* The echo of the childhood game Hide and Seek reverberated in his brain along with the fear and excitement that always accompanied it: *Coming, ready or not!*

# Chapter 8

"Where do I start this investigation?" Hunter asked himself out loud as he drove back to Shannon's house.

When Hunter turned the antique doorbell, this time Charles opened it with Shannon right behind him. "Hunter," she said as they walked to the living room and sat down, "Why is so much happening out here? Damn! Maybe you need to just move in. You know Charles must have a photographic memory, right?" She turned to the child. "Tell him everything you told me. I'm proud of you. You gave a great description."

Charles looked at Shannon out of the corner of his eye. When she reached over and gave him a hug, he snuggled close to her. "Let's go sit at the kitchen table," said Shannon. A glass of milk and a few chocolate chip cookies later, everyone was more relaxed. Karla and Tippiny came in and sat in the chairs around the kitchen table. Hunter smiled at seeing this small family bond. He let them revel in the moment, took out his cellphone, laid it on the kitchen table, and pulled out his notebook.

"Okay, Charles," he said. "I'm writing down what you tell me. Take your time and describe what you saw. Don't leave anything out; every little thing is important." He opened the notebook on the kitchen table, pencil in hand. "Go ahead; I'm ready."

Straightening in his seat, Charles realized all eyes were on him and took a deep breath. "Well, I was standing behind Shannon between Tippiny and Karla. Everyone was bigger than me, so I couldn't see anything. Then I heard a loud noise, you know like the Fourth of July or New Year's? People started running everywhere. I was looking for Karla when somebody bumped into me. Then she fell to the ground. She said a really bad word, Shannon said I could not say it, but it begins with…"

"Whoa! You said *she*. Do you think it was a woman?"

Charles' head bobbed up and down.

"Why?"

"Her voice sounded like a woman's. Besides, she had little hands, but no paint on her fingernails like Shannon's. Her hood dropped off when she fell, and her brown hair was messy, and she smelled bad. Shannon would never let us out the door if we looked like that. I saw her eyes; they were dark brown with black make-up all around them. I know I saw a lady."

"How did you see it that quickly?" Hunter asked. *Boy, Charles does have a photographic memory.*

"She stumbled trying to get up while everyone was running away. The bag she had fell between us and she looked right at me and it grabbed it like I was going to take it away from her. I didn't know if it was the urn, 'cause I couldn't see, till after she was gone. The bag was dark blue. She pulled it open and when she looked inside, she smiled. That's when I noticed how little her hands were. She had a pretty ring."

*Aha, it sounds like the urn wasn't broken.* "You *are* observant. What else did you see?" Hunter asked.

"She can run fast. She got up and held that bag close. If I had known who she was or what was in the bag, I would have grabbed it. "

"It's okay that you didn't try to get the bag. What about clothes, Charles? What color were they, and shoes?"

"Black boots, fancy with gold chains. Not rain boots. She wore a black hoodie, pants and shirt, too, with long sleeves. I saw the shirt's collar was white."

"How tall do you think she was? Was she fat or skinny?"

"Maybe about as tall as Shannon but skinnier." Hunter glanced towards Shannon, who had put on a few pounds as she settled into the Delta.

*That would make her about five feet-five, weighing perhaps a hundred and ten pounds.* Hunter leaned over toward the young boy. "Anything else?"

Charles nodded. "Yeah, she was kind of soft when she ran into me. And," he pushed up his shirtsleeve, "her ring scratched my arm." A scratch proved his point.

"Did you see the ring?"

"Barely, but it was sharp."

"What color was the stone?"

"Dark red, and it stuck up kind of high."

*Garnet, if it's a birthstone, it's a clue that she could have been born in January, like me.* He scratched his ear. *This is almost too much detail to be true. Charles' memory sure seems intact, but I need to check it out.*

Hunter faked a cough. When Shannon left to get him some water, he turned to Charles. "Was that lady wearing a blue sweatshirt like Shannon's?"

Charles wrinkled his brow. "Shannon's shirt isn't blue, it's brown. It's not even a sweatshirt. It has buttons. I told you the lady wore a BLACK hoodie."

"Okay, never mind." *Charles was observant and his memory was on target.*

Shannon soon returned with more than water. She had a tray of glasses, sandwiches, chips and dip, cookies, and a pitcher of lemonade and everyone piled around the table. "Thought you might like lunch since you have been here so long. Levenia brought the leftover food here. We may as well use it."

While they nibbled on the food and drank lemonade, Hunter asked Charles a few more questions and nothing significant came up. He also questioned Shannon, but she'd kept her attention on where the noise came from and getting the kids to safety. She didn't see the perpetrator at all.

When they finished, everyone moved to the living room. Karla sat next to her brother on the sofa, she had nothing to offer but a shrug. Shannon said she'd held onto Karla's hand during the entire incident and beyond as they returned home. Without other possibilities of help, Hunter left satisfied with the information he'd received. It was a good start.

Next, Hunter visited the minister, after calling ahead to be sure he was available to talk. He made a short drive to the church. The pastor met him at the door and invited Hunter in. It took only a few minutes for Hunter to see little hope of getting anywhere. The old man told him, "I didn't even realize there was an explosion. My hearing is failing. First thing I knew, someone—it looked like a little white kid—snatched the urn and ran. I called out for help, but I don't think anyone heard me in the commotion."

Hunter made an effort. "Can you remember anything? Did the person have a weapon? What about clothes?"

The pastor shook his head. "Looked like a young man, kind of small built. Nothing else comes to mind. My eyesight's not too good either. So, I'm afraid I can't give you a description of the person. It all happened so quickly."

Hunter thanked the pastor for his time and left with exactly what he expected–zero information. He returned to the office to absorb what he'd been told, sort things out, and make a plan.

Like a rabbit hopping along on a trail, Hunter wrote down two names–Dallas Devil and Frederica. Under each heading, he made a pro and con list of why each one might be the thief of the urn, or not. Then he scratched out *Frederica,* realizing that was a stupid idea. Charles would have recognized his own mother.

Hunter pulled out a couple of news clips from a folder he brought from Dallas and thumbed through them. He also took out a small booklet and checked a couple of ideas about the Devil. *I'm an anachronism. Everyone else takes notes on their cell phone nowadays, but not me. I've even got an extra notebook in my pocket.*

He opened the book and flipped back a few pages to his old notes. He spotted a list of four names marked *Persons of Interest;* one he'd made after the second child's murder. His brain whirled as he recalled the interviews with possible suspects. The first man, the one who found the body, had been released. He cringed seeing second name; the one who'd been incarcerated unjustly.

The third made him chuckle. When they brought in that subject, a husky voice and crew cut hairstyle with uneven edges fooled them. The flat-chested person spent the night in the men's section of the jail and made no complaints. In the morning, a male guard noticed the subject sitting down to go to the bathroom had missing parts and reported they may have a female. After checking they discovered he was right. The new guard who missed the obvious was put on leave immediately.

When Hunter looked at his, or her, records, he noticed her name was so unusual that he had to write it down to remember it, Rapier Fogg. He remembered her swearing and demanding her phone call. She wanted to contact her wealthy parents.

He sat with her as she made the call and bragged about the family's money being made in oil. No one answered, but she left a message. Hunter's team tried to interview Rapier, but she refused to say anything until she had an attorney.

Her parents arrived early the following morning, with a lawyer, and Hunter knew the man—one of the most expensive and sleazy attorneys money could buy.

"Where's my baby girl?" Rapier's buxom mother demanded, slamming her Brahmin handbag on the counter.

Their lawyer spoke up. "I insist on seeing my client immediately," he said.

Hunter could hear them in the front lobby of the station, but he stayed in the back, letting his staff deal with them.

Her father's voice boomed out, "You git her right now, or you'll face a false arrest charge. You hear me?" He pulled out his wallet. "We're bailin' her out. This here's my lawyer, in case. My baby didn't kill nobody and don't you think 'bout giving me any trouble." The lawyer nodded and asked about the charge.

Hunter came out and explained they'd brought her in on a charge of loitering. She was seen on a store camera near the site of the crime. Then he made an admission. He'd gotten word that the image was blurry and a charge against Rapier wouldn't hold up. They had to release her since there wasn't evidence linking her to the death.

Rapier appeared with a sneer on her face, possessions in hand, and ready to leave. Hunter noticed she accepted her mother's hug but she left her own arms hanging by her side. Not a hint of a smile crossed her face.

"Sorry, honey. We didn't see your message until this morning, or we'd have come to get you sooner." Her mother handed her a sleeve of Snickers candy bars. "I brought your favorite. Eat one; it'll make you feel better."

Without a thank you, Rapier ripped open the package, removed one candy bar, and bit into it, dropping the wrapper on the floor.

Rapier's father accosted her with a growl. "We shouldn't a come to git ya atal. You been missing for months. Ain't heard a word from ya." He took a deep breath. "Had yo' mama desperate to find you." He got close to her face. "You ain't nothin' but trouble. Not like yo' little sister Callie. I wish you'd been the one—"

Rapier's mother piped up. "Stop it! She tried to save--"

Fogg glared at his wife saying, "Shut up!" Following his order, she hung her head. He gripped his daughter's arm and all three headed for the door. "Now you goin' home and you'll stay there, y'hear?"

Rapier curled her lip and remained as silent as she had during interviews.

"Don't give me no sass. I see that de-fiant expression. Looka here, Girl, we'll hog tie ya if we hafta." Still ranting, he dragged her out of hearing distance.

Hunter wrinkled his brow. *What did all that mean? How does it fit with what is going on now? Oh, Hell! I thought we convicted the right guy then. Could this be the suspect, and the same person who snatched the urn?*

Hunter ran his fingers through his hair. A contradiction formed in his mind. *We made a mistake before. I don't want to do it again. It is interesting about the little sister, Callie, I wonder...* He made a mental note, it was time to fill in another person in the office on what was going on. While he was good at figuring things out, Officer Chan had the best research skills and technology experience of anyone in the office. Rapier was rather young, barely in her twenties; if she been arrested as a minor and that had been covered up, he'd unearth it. For now, he moved on.

With a sigh, he studied the last name on the list. The case against that homeless man who spent the night behind the dumpster was weak. He, too, was released quickly. What a mess. The arrest of the wrong man and three other people questioned led to zero as it turned out. He slipped the booklet back into the folder. *Instead of getting better at my job with age and experience, I feel like I'm getting worse. What the Hell makes me keep doing this?* He slipped on his winter jacket he took from the back of his chair, put on his hat, and headed for the door. *Maybe I should turn in my badge.*

# Chapter 9

When the alarm awakened him the next morning, Hunter had renewed resolve. He hopped out of bed, fed King his breakfast, made coffee, and sipped on it with a revitalized determination. The Dallas Devil wasn't going to outwit him. No, Sir. Failure had to be conquered and he was man enough to stay the course and make that happen, no matter how long it took. The ringing of his cell phone jolted his senses. He answered with a gruff, "Sheriff Harley."

In a breathless voice, Carlton, his smart-aleck deputy, blurted out, "Sheriff, I've got TERRIBLE news. You know that old cotton bin on the Tollar Plantation next to Shannon's house? Well, she found a body in a pile of debris along the side of the building. It's where the wall faces away from her house."

He continued, "She thought she heard a car out there early this morning but didn't go check because it was dark. When she did go to see what was going on, she saw a child's leg unearthed. She knew there had to be a body under there and called 911." Nonplussed, Carlton was far from his usual confident self. "I…I'm standing here looking at it. I need you out here. What should I do?" His voice shook on every syllable.

"Don't touch anything. I'm on my way." Hunter called the Bolivar County Medical Examiner and left his home with siren blaring. When he arrived at Shannon's home he hopped out of his car. Even this weathered lawman reacted to the sad, grizzly scene. One of his officers brought out a video recorder to capture anything they might miss The Medical Examiner observed as Carlton slowly removed the boards, revealing the child underneath. Hunter saw the child's blonde hair mixed with the dirt from the ground. When Carlton removed the final board covering her face, he saw she couldn't be more than seven years old. *So, the Devil couldn't control himself.*

The Medical Examiner kept a stone-like face during the examination of the body. He looked for signs of trauma and other evidence to prove a natural death; however, foul play was suspected. Even those two seasoned officers stood gritting their teeth at the heart-breaking scene. The only comfort was the death was recent and due to the cold weather, decomposition had not started to the point where they could see it.

Hunter stooped to check the body. He gasped when he noticed one lock of hair had been cut off from the child's head. A confirmation to his fears, Hunter stepped away for a minute to regain his composure.

The Medical Examiner commented, "Her body is still intact, but you can see bruise marks on her small body. She must have gotten them before she died. They cover her arms and forehead. Her clothes are threadbare, worn rags, but still intact. I think this is the cause of death." He pointed to a thin, red ligature mark encircling her throat.

Hunter cringed as they examined the area around the child's body. He slipped on plastic gloves. Brushing aside some of the dirt and debris remaining on her body, he lifted one of her hands to find her little finger broken. He wiped mud from her cheek and stared at the round face. His face reddened when he stared at her slanted eyes that were partially open and turned to the Medical Examiner.

The man nodded. "Yes, she's a Downs Syndrome child, even more vulnerable than other children.

Hunter stood and turned to his deputy, "Carlton, I want you to escort the ambulance when the Medical Examiner removes the body. I'm going to talk to Shannon, but I'll be right back."

"Yes, sir," said Carlton. He was quiet and Hunter saw how pale he was. *Welcome to the saddest part of this job, kid.*

Speculative thoughts and questions raced through Hunter's brain. Who was this child? He saw a lot of the local kids when invited to speak to the first through fifth graders at Cleveland's Elementary school, but he didn't remember a Down's Syndrome child. However, Zita knew everybody in Cleveland. She'd know. He wrinkled his nose, realizing nobody reported a kid missing in the last few days…months actually. How did the Dallas Devil get her here and why? The beast committed a heinous crime against this defenseless little girl. His brain whirled.

Standing up and then turning his head away from the victim and looking towards the river to clear it, he walked around the corner of the cotton bin and spotted Shannon standing in the doorway of the Tollar house, flanked by Charles and Karla. With a solemn expression on her pale face, she gave a wave while shaking her head. He understood her perplexity and didn't approach right away, giving her time to regain her composure before asking her about this new trauma. He couldn't tell her his suspicions, but he needed to know what she witnessed.

He straightened his shoulders and headed toward the house. As he neared his destination, Shannon shooed the two children away, telling them, "Go upstairs and play. I'll call you when you can come back down."

For once, Charles didn't give her an argument. Hunter sighed in relief. He was in no mood to deal with that. "Good Morning, Shannon," he said, realizing what a misstatement that was–the morning was anything but good.

Leaning against the door frame, Shannon's chin dropped to her chest. "Oh, Hunter, this is so horrible. It's the worst thing I've ever experienced. Even Goldie's remains were stolen…why is everything terrible happening out here? I came here to provide a stable life for Charles and Karla, not to deal with thieves and murders." Pulling a tissue from her pocket, she wiped tears from the corners of her eyes with shaky fingers. "That poor little child. My God, how she must have suffered!"

Hunter patted her shoulder. "I hate to do this, but let's talk. Could we go inside?"

They went into the living room. Hunter sat in a chair and Shannon plopped on the loveseat opposite him. "Tell me exactly what has happened since I left yesterday," Hunter said.

Taking a deep breath, Shannon related the sequence of events. "The day was normal. One of your deputies came to look for more evidence in the field, I worked on my computer, the kids played in the yard, but not by the tree, out in the big field. I watched them from my office window in case anything else happened. It was past eleven p.m. last night when I heard some noise, like a car bottoming out at the dips in the front road. I went to the window to see but it was too dark, but something was moving near the cotton bin. I thought it was locals hanging out or kids looking for a place to make out. When I turned on the porch light, they got in the car in a hurry. They sped off towards Highway 8."

She cupped her chin with both hands. "This morning, when I got close to where I saw them last night, I could see, oh damn, I could see the little child's leg under the pile of old lumber. It was horrible! I've never, oh, I knew she was dead." This time, she didn't try to stop the flow of tears; she sobbed aloud. Hanging her head, she blurted out, "Who could have done this? Who's that child?"

Hunter went over, sat beside her, and put his arm around her shoulder. His brain raced. "We uncovered her face. Did you know the child had Down's Syndrome?" he asked. A loud outcry testified to Shannon's sorrow. "How in the world could anyone, even the worst monster, do this to a defenseless kid like that?" She swirled to face Hunter. "You've got to find him and punish him, or her. Damn it all, I wondered if this could be Fredrica's dirty work, but she wouldn't have a real motive, unless she just wanted to terrify me." She made a fist and hit Hunter's shoulder. "And no matter who did this, I'd like to be the prosecutor. I'd punish him to the fullest extent of the law. Execution would be too good for him, but I'd find a place like Hell to put him for the rest of his life."

"I understand. But right now…ummm… we don't know who the killer is. Matter of fact, we don't know who the child is, either. Have you seen her before?" It wasn't the time to tell her who he suspected. Only Zita knew the real story, but that might have to change soon.

Shannon jumped to her feet. "No but find out!"

Hunter stood, too. "We will. Zita's on her way and I bet she'll at least know who the child is." He looked out the window "Ah, I think that's her now."

Hunter told Shannon, "You can't do anything. Leave it all to us and keep an eye on the children. I bet they're upset. Kids instinctively know when something's amiss. Go calm them down and then try to get some rest." He headed for the door. "I'll keep you posted."

Hunter hurried out and toward Zita's patrol car, mouthing a prayer that Zita would be able to identify the child. Then they could move on with a hunt for the murderer–a man he'd wish the same fate upon as Shannon did. A light flashed in his brain–all the assumptions related to a man, but could it be a woman? It wasn't impossible. Almost anyone would have the strength to use a rope to strangle that small, mentally challenged child who may also have been disabled. His depressing thoughts of inadequacy resurfaced. *Is this another case I won't be able to solve? Life is so unfair.*

# Chapter 10

Zita's gripped hands and white knuckles were the only outward signs of the repugnance she felt when she stared at the little girl silent in death. "That's Allie, little Allie Lewis. She lived with her grandmother in an old farmhouse between here and the Tollar plantation. I only saw her a few times at the store; they didn't go out much. Allie was a friendly little girl. She couldn't tell you ten dimes were in a dollar, but she remembered my name every time I saw her." She took a deep breath and glanced towards Hunter, "I can't believe …umm… anyone would harm her."

Hunter nodded, "We didn't have reports of a child being missing. Why wouldn't she report it to us?"

"Ila Lewis, her grandma, was a private person, almost a recluse. I'm guessing she might have early signs of dementia. Remember we got a call from the Popes; she and Allie were walking down the middle of the road, ignoring the few cars that passed. Carlton drove out to check on them, the lady was confused. Allie was able to tell him their car was at the gas station and he drove them back to it. Mrs. Lewis' remembered where she was and said it happens sometimes when she takes her medication. Told Carlton she was going to call her doctor, so he let them be on their way. Allie is…was...about seven years old. I think it happened a few months ago and no one has heard anything since."

She shook her head. "It's sad. Mrs. Lewis was a nurse and a midwife in Texas, not sure what town, before she moved here a few years ago. Levenia, who knows all the gossip, said Ms. Lewis adopted Allie when she was six months old. Her mamma took off when she realized the baby was disabled. Allie was left to her son Billy, who didn't care about his child either, and so Ila took her. Levenia also said Billy was trying to be a blues musician, but I don't think it went anywhere. You have to have a soul to play the blues. If you abandon your child, then you ain't got a soul."

"Okay, let's take your car to Mrs. Lewis' house. She's next of kin, so we need to notify her about Allie's death. Maybe we'll get lucky and catch her in a lucid minute and, if she knows, she can clue us in to what happened."

*　　*　　*

Zita had dropped off a food basket at Mrs. Lewis' home a few months ago, so she knew exactly where to go. At the dilapidated house, Hunter banged on the front door. No answer. He tried again without luck. "Wait here," he told Zita as he left to circle the house. As he did, he saw no signs of life. Faded curtains with ragged edges blocked his view inside. But one had a big hole and he peeked through it to spot a woman lying crosswise on a bed. He went to the back door and knocked. When nobody answered, he wriggled the knob and it popped open. A foul smell filled his nostrils. Holding his nose, Hunter went straight to the bedroom where he saw a woman lying down. It was clear she had been dead for a while. He touched her arm; it was cold.. As he walked down the hall to the front door to let Zita in, he saw a child's shoe and a jacket ripped in a way that would happen if it was pulled off. He called out, "Is anyone here?" Nothing.

Zita followed him to the bedroom and stated, "She's clearly deceased." Pulling on plastic gloves, she touched the woman's arm. "Notice that smell? Been dead a while from the rigidity of her body, but I'm no expert. Man, we're going to keep the medical examiner busy today, aren't we?"

Hunter nodded. "She's on top of the spread. I looked for a rope mark on her neck, like Allie's and I don't see any evidence of foul play. She's lying across the bed, so it looks like she just fell there."

"The house is a bit of a mess. You reckon the killer was kidnapping the kid and Ila tried to stop her? She was so frail; it wouldn't take much."

"Could be." Hunter called for his officers to send an ambulance and the forensics team on his cell phone and then turned to Zita. "We'll wait to see what they have to say. Meanwhile, let's see what we can find out."

The pair to the child's shoe kicked in the corner was a clue but not much of one. They checked closets but they contained old clothes. Medication for high blood pressure and an unopened bottle of pills prescribed for dementia was in the bathroom medicine cabinet. Dirty laundry piled on top of an old washing machine reeked. The refrigerator had half empty shelves. A jar of mayonnaise, a quart of sour milk, and a bottle of ranch salad dressing with an expired date sat alone on one shelf. Half a head of lettuce was brown and a partial loaf of bread with mold all through it sat alone on another. It was a wonder the two occupants didn't die of food poisoning. Zita retrieved a sliver of a candy wrapper from under a chair. She looked at Hunter and made a face that said more than words. By the time they finished, help had arrived.

After the other officers arrived at the house Hunter and Zita returned to the office, there was nothing else they could do. Their two-man, part-time forensics team was working both of the scenes and they had to wait to see what the evidence revealed, if anything.  Wanting time to sort out what he could, he sent Zita home. Then he also left. He needed time to think.

But he didn't go home. He knew V was keeping an eye on King, so instead, he headed nearby to where Goldie's body had washed up, in its own way, the catalyst of everything happening now. Maybe he could revive the spirit of Goldie Parsons or Mama Cheche. Two more mysterious deaths in one day had his mind boggled. He needed help–maybe from the supernatural–the mojo. He scratched his head. *But I don't believe in the mojo; I DON'T.*

Hunter drove past Mama Cheche's house, but he didn't stop. He couldn't quite give in to superstition. He did slow down. If Mama really had powers, she'd manifest them somehow. Nothing happened. With a sigh, he turned around, and went to the Sunflower River.

When he reached the river, an orange sun was settling on the horizon. Big and bright, it made Hunter aware of his own smallness, one creature on Earth amongst millions. *How many of us make any lasting impact? Do we fail to achieve? Do we leave this Earth a better place than we found it? Only a few do, and only a few are remembered long after death. Which category do I fit into? Ha, that's an easy question.*

The growling of his stomach made him aware that he hadn't eaten all day. But all he was really hungry for were answers to the mounting questions this so-called peaceful town had thrust upon him. *Why didn't I stay in Dallas? Looks like life would've been simpler there. No, I couldn't face failure. My pride took over. I wanted a chance to redeem myself. I still do.*

*But damn it all, it shouldn't be this tough! God, give me a chance!*

His attention was drawn to the sun. He stared at it and could have sworn it shook as it dropped lower. It reminded him of a story Zita told him about Catholic priest visiting Medjugorje saying he saw the sun shake. Then another phenomenon occurred. His eyes seemed pulled to the water where, in clouds above it, a figure formed. Hunter shook his head. He'd seen such forms in the sky before, elephants, dogs, but never one that called to mind Mama Cheche. Just a coincidence. Not true. She wasn't trying to tell him anything. But his gaze stayed focused on the cloud and in a part that looked like a hand, he saw an object. Was it a stone?

Hunter forced his gaze back to the car's steering wheel and he turned the key in the ignition. *I've got to get out of here. I'm having strange thoughts and I'm seeing things. I'm tired; I need some rest–a way to get my mind back on track. Whew! I'm glad I'm alone. I could never explain this.*

He drove away from the scene of Goldie's body washing up after sixty years, but not before he turned on the radio and heard the announcement, "Another crime is being investigated today in our area, but we have scanty information…"

Hunter switched off the news, but he couldn't switch off his brain which kept telling him, *The murder of the child, an old woman, and the theft of the urn are connected. It had to be the Dallas Devil, but how to catch the criminal? If I'm the prey that person wants….* Those thoughts persisted, but he couldn't account for where they came from. And every time the word *Mojo* popped into his head suggesting it was responsible, he pushed it out. Still, despite his strenuous efforts, sensibility failed to preside.

# Chapter 11

The next morning, Hunter finally confessed to Chan what had happened in Dallas, and entrusted him with digging into the past. It touched his heart to find Chan supportive and willing to help out anyway possible. When he was mulling over what might come of Chan's research on Rapier Fogg, he got a text from Zita. She said Whiskers, the proprietor of Wally's Gas-n-Go, found an odd message in his restroom, and that Hunter needed to come by to take a look. Whiskers said he'd lock up the bathroom till the sheriff got there.

Caught up on paperwork, Hunter drove out to the gas station. When he pulled up near the door, noticing the age of the gas station and the classic worn out look not unusual in the Delta, Hunter thought, *I bet the food in the place is out of this world. You can always find good food in Southern gas stations.*

A whiff of fried chicken tickled his nose as he entered the store. It was too late for breakfast, but too early for lunch, so the place had no other customers at the time. He held out his hand to the man behind the counter, he had seen him at Levenia's diner in the past.

Hunter noticed the ridge on the tall man's bulbous nose. It made a path connecting one side of his face with more lines than a road map to the other. Repressing a grin, he could see why they called the man Whiskers. He had a salt and pepper beard stretching almost to his waist. It was long, but well-groomed.

"I've heard a lot about you, but we haven't officially met. I'm Sheriff Harley," he said, "and I understand they call you Whiskers."

"They do." Whiskers stroked his beard. Locking the cash register, he came around the counter. "I called 'cause there's something  you ought to see, Sheriff. Just follow me."

"I guess you couldn't see which restroom, Ladies or Men's, the person who left the note went into."

"Har, har, didn't have to. We only have one. We were unisex before the term was coined."

He opened the door and pointed to a mirror with a piece of paper taped onto it. "Didn't touch a thing."

Slipping on gloves, Harley leaned over the sink to read what was printed on the paper in large capital letters with terrible handwriting: *Grandmas fault. That kid was going with me till she tried to stop us. Kid made it worst. Couldn't stop the brat from screaming. Had to kill her. You next Sherrif.*

As he gingerly removed the note, he avoided touching the tape. He saw long, blonde hairs that looked the same shade as Allie's. If any fingerprints were available, he didn't want to contaminate them. Next, Hunter made a mental note of the three grammatical errors—no apostrophe in Grandma's, worst, instead of worse, and the misspelling of Sheriff. It revealed that either the Devil wasn't educated, or the mistakes were deliberate. Hunter suspected it was a lack of education. He slipped the note into a plastic bag, along with a couple of strands of blonde hair attached to the tape. That gave him a connection: cutting and keeping the lock of  hair as a trophy was the Method of Operation of the Dallas Devil.

"Did you see this person?" Hunter asked.

"Nope, but the damn devil had to be the one who stole the restroom key while I straightened some shelves. But he didn't put it back. Now I have to pay a locksmith for another key."

"Damn devil" was probably an accurate description. Wait! Did he know anything? If so, then so did Levenia. Damn! It might already be all over town! Hunter had to put his fears aside and focus. This matched the work of the Dallas Devil. Hunter continued his interrogation. "Was he in a car? Did he buy gas?"

"Funny, he pulled up at a pump while I was going to the shelves and stayed out of my sight. I looked up how he paid. Used a Visa gift card, you know the ones you can buy at the dollar store" He clicked his tongue. "When he drove off in that dirty old gray Lumina, though, I got the last two numbers of his muddied tag–25. That mean anything?"

"It could. I'll check it out." He gave a finger salute and walked out of the store to his car.

Hunter headed back to his home first with a box of fried chicken. The lunch was wonderful, and King enjoyed the bits Hunter dropped in his bowl. His first action would be to get the note and the hair checked for DNA. His thoughts wandered. Now he knew the killer had a car, a gray Chevrolet Lumina. Was he sleeping in it at night in a remote field in the Delta? There were a couple of empty houses around Cleveland; he could be using them, a barn, or outbuilding. *Wait a minute. I saw an old barn covered with vines in the backyard of Ila Lewis' house. She had a car at one point. Hmm–I'll check it out.*

His thoughts turned to other questions. Did the killer take baths? Maybe not, since Charles remembered the person who stole the urn smelled bad. He'd messaged everyone to be on the lookout for the gray Lumina, and maybe a deputy on patrol would spot something. He had those last numbers of the car tag; it might result in a clue. But maybe not. This guy was slick. *I keep thinking "Guy" but I know it might be a woman.* Hunter blew out his breath, once again wondering, *I had options for a job. Why the Hell did I ever choose to move to Cleveland?*

*    *    *

Chan had returned to the office from Ila Lewis' house by the time Hunter arrived. He'd checked the old barn and found fresh tire tracks, but no car. "Mrs. Lewis was seen driving around town; she had access to a car, so I checked on it. It's kind of strange," Chan said, "Nobody has seen her driving that car for months, until the other day."

"Did they know she was the person at the wheel? Did they see the little girl? Where was it?"

"A woman who lives down the road a piece from her saw her pass by in the dusty Lumina. Cleveland is a small town; you can't drive anywhere without someone noticing. Ha, ha, she called Mrs. Lewis 'Looney.' It was the first time she'd seen the old woman in ages. She said the head and face was almost covered with a hood, but some gray hair poked out on her forehead." He held up both palms. "Funny, Mrs. Lewis' hair was very thin judging from her corpse. Didn't look like enough there to stick out."

"Maybe she wore a wig." suggested Hunter.

"Didn't see one anywhere." Chan sat on the edge of Hunter's desk. "Here is the juicy stuff. As part of my officer training, we were taught to search every nook and cranny for drugs and such. When we pulled out the drawer on the dresser, it stuck a bit. So we turned it over and found a couple of letters taped on the bottom. You're not going to believe this, but the return address on one was Dallas." He pulled out a plastic bag containing two envelopes and handed it to Hunter. "Take a look."

Retrieving plastic gloves from his desk drawer, Hunter took out one envelope addressed to Mrs. Ila Lewis, opened it, and pulled out two pieces of paper, two birth certificates. He read the names of the parents and thought, *Well, I'll be damned.*

# Chapter 12

Hunter and Chan could not deny the coincidence when they saw the mailing address on the letters. It was another resource to help his deputy find more information. The sheriff asked Chan to keep searching to check to see if there was any way the address was tied to Rapier Fogg.

The next day, Chan came into Hunter's office, his face was beaming. "I know you like things on paper, so I printed the important parts out, but the rest in an email I sent to you," he said. "I found a high school yearbook with Rapier's picture in it." He held up a picture of a girl with a grim expression on her face, and a close-cropped haircut. "Rapier Fogg" was the only thing written under it, no achievements, no clubs, no interests.

Chan pointed to the picture above. "From the address on the envelopes, I found the local high school. They just had a ten year reunion and guess who was on the list of graduates? Rapier Fogg! It was easy to find the yearbook and photo. I got in touch with this girl, "Diane Bolden. She was the person organizing the class reunion and had her phone number as the contact on the list. Boy, is she a talker! She said Rapier was a loner who always sat in the back of the room and rarely spoke unless asked a question, which she always answered correctly."

He took a deep breath. "They worked together at a sandwich shop. Even though Rapier didn't communicate much,

Diane invited Rapier to her wedding, hoping it would draw her out. It didn't help; she refused." He raised his chin. "When Rapier didn't show up for work one day, Diane went to her house to see what was wrong. Oh, man, did she get the surprise of her life. Nobody answered the door, so she went around the back of the house. She saw a man digging a deep hole. He turned and glared at her screaming, 'What do you want? Get out of here, or you'll wish you had. And don't go blabbing about this, y'hear?' She said he ran toward her, with the shovel raised above his head. It came down hard on the ground near her feet.

Chan paused. "I asked Diane if she knew what was going on then. Her voice shook when she said, 'It looked like Mr. Fogg was digging a grave. All I could think of was Rapier's little sister Callie. Whenever Rapier mentioned Callie, she'd rant about what a pest she was. She even said something weird like *We got rid of the retarded girl when she was born. I'll take care of this one sooner or later.'* I couldn't help but wonder if she'd done that. It made me sick that she called her 'retarded.' That's so insensitive!"

"I asked her who she told about that incident. Her eyes got wide as saucers. Nobody. Mr. Fogg has a reputation. Rumors circulated that he had a Fixer who'd kill for him if ordered to do so. Rapier had a reputation, too. She once punched out a guy who bumped into her and knocked her down in the hallway at school."

Chan looked at the sheriff. "She said she was too afraid to tell anybody back then."

Chan looked at his boss. "It's a stretch, but I think there's a tie-in with Rapier and this little girl Allie's murder. Where do we go from here, Sheriff?"

"Hmm–this is complex. Won't be a simple answer." Hunter stood and squared his shoulders. "Let me check with Roy. Maybe he has some new information on the Foggs. I'll give him an update and get his views on this. Then, we can take it from there." Hunter knew it was a put-off, but he needed time to study this before committing to a course of action. Dismissing his deputy with a walk to the door, he said, "Keep digging. Somebody else may know something. I'll get back to you as soon as I can."

Hunter didn't get much sleep that night. Tossing and turning, the word "they" flitted through his brain. So did his intuition that Allie's murder and the theft of the urn were connected. But the dots wouldn't fit together. *Allie has to be the retard. But she was just killed. Who got rid of her? When? She was Mrs. Lewis' granddaughter—"*

Hunter sat up in bed. *Was she really? Mrs. Lewis was a midwife and she once lived in Dallas.* Exhausted, he flopped back onto his pillow. *Those thoughts are too crazy. I've got to get some rest. I will give Roy a call tomorrow to see if Rapier shows up in any other records. Maybe she was caught doing something illegal since I left. Maybe we can make some sense of it.* He closed his eyes and forced sleep to consume him.

His first phone call the next day didn't produce any results. Roy didn't answer. Two hours later, Hunter's call was returned. "What's up, Old Buddy? Are you hot on a trail?"

"You tell me after I tell you what I've found out." He related the details of Chan's interview with Diane and quoted the statement credited to Rapier. Then he asked, "What do you know about the Foggs?"

"Ha, that's on point. As you already know, Bruno Fogg made big money in oil. He is very powerful. And he's ruthless.

We haven't been able to pin anything on him, but he's got a fixer all right."

"I know some of it, but I was out with the flu for a week then. Only time I was ever sick enough to miss work. Do you think you can get the records on Rapier's birth? More importantly, how about Callie's? See if a midwife named Ila Lewis was involved."

"Where are you going with this, Hunter? Oh, yeah, I had to take over while you were gone. I can check on those records, if there are any."

"What do you mean?"

"I recall trying to find information on Callie's birth when she died. It happened under questionable circumstances. She fell into their swimming pool. When we got wind of it and questioned the Foggs, the parents claimed Rapier tried to pull her out, but it was too late. They evaded all the issues including where Callie was buried. We couldn't prove anything but it looked more like that kid was drowned deliberately. I can send you more details." He paused. "The odd thing was that we couldn't find any birth certificate for Callie."

"Uh, huh. So, she wasn't born in a hospital?"

"No, and we tried to check with Mrs. Lewis. She'd moved away by then and we couldn't find out where, until now. So, she's in Cleveland, right?"

"She was. She's dead now, and the child that was in her care is dead. It might be the work of the Dallas Devil. The story around here is that she adopted the little girl when her son got a girl pregnant and didn't want to care for the disabled child."

"What? That can't be right. I'm looking at the folder we have on Ms. Ila Lewis and she does not have a husband, or a child, listed. She doesn't have any surviving relatives, either. I remember because we had no contacts to search her down. Not even friends or neighbors. She was a loner who made her living as a midwife. She lived in a tiny, one room apartment behind a house owned by a man who said she'd slip the rent under his door and he rarely ever saw her. He didn't know she vacated the place until she didn't pay rent the first of the month."

"I see. That kind of woman could be paid off to hide most anything," Hunter replied.

"She sure could. Look, I'll email those records. I know you Hunter. I can tell you've got some ideas. Give them a hard look and let me know what you come up with."

"Will do." Hunter hung up and got busy. He took out a sheet of typing paper and turned it sideways, to make a chart. On top, he made columns listing members of the Fogg family, with the word "Unknown" heading up one of them. Then he added Ina Lewis, Billy, and Allie. Scrawling information under each name, he tacked it to a pegboard on his office wall and stood back to study it.

Zita came in and blurted out, "What is this?"

"Sit down, Zita, and I'll tell you about it."

For the next thirty minutes, Hunter talked, and Zita listened. When he was done, she said, "You know what, Hunter, you may just be onto something."

Her reassurance encouraged him. Whether his speculation was wrong or right, he was determined to find out. The likelihood of sleepless nights didn't deter Hunter. He was on a mission and he'd pursue it to the death. The devil be damned!

# Chapter 13

Hunter looked at the three things closely related to a murder–Motivation, Opportunity, and Method. He found it odd that the first letters of those words spelled MOM. Most moms wouldn't murder their own child. Even Ila would not murder her grandchild.

Hunter scratched his head. In this case, it was certain Ila didn't harm her charge. He knew it was the Dallas Devil. Ila died before Allie, so the Devil could have killed her first. Back to motivation, he let his thoughts fly. Money wasn't involved as far as he could tell, unless Ila was blackmailing somebody, or she was being blackmailed. But why and who? Could Billy have anything to do with this? He picked up the phone and called Roy.

"Hey, man," he said, "I have a few questions for you. Can you see if you have any records on a Billy Lewis? Let me tell you what I've found out first. It came from Levenia. That gal knows everything around here, if you know what I mean. She told me she remembered Billy. He was a wanna be blues singer who lived in Dallas with his mother Ila Lewis. He moved here to play in the local blues bars, make connections, and become famous. He also tried his luck in Memphis, but no such luck. He wasn't worth a flip as a singer and the guys who were good told him so. He never sang a note at Ground Zero in Clarksdale. Story goes that he went back to Memphis and got deep into drugs. But he lied and told his mama he was making a name for himself in

Cleveland. That's why she moved here but learned the truth too late. That's all the info I could get."

"Roy, if this is the case, then Mrs. Lewis did have children, she had a son, and he came to Cleveland. Your records have to be wrong." Hunter told him.

"Interesting, let me check to see if a Billy Lewis is in the system." In short order, Roy brought up Billy's records and shared what he discovered with Hunter, "We hauled Billy in once for intoxication. The report says he got drunk and wanted to play at the blues bar, but they wouldn't let him. You're on target with what you told me, by the way. Billy did live with his mama here in Dallas, she was his contact on the arrest record. Things were settled out of court and then we don't know where he went afterwards. Looks like he ventured to Mississippi and Tennessee."

"Hunter, I am not sure…wait, let me check something…" said Roy as Hunter heard the frantic clicks on the keyboard.

"Yes!" exclaimed Roy, "I just put in William Lewis, not Billy Lewis and guess what popped up? A death record."

"What?" asked Hunter, confused.

Roy continued, "Seems like he came back to Dallas and the next thing you know, he was killed in a fight outside the bar he was arrested at previously. Never even had a suspect for the murderer. They did an autopsy and found his system full of cocaine and liquor. I guess because of the name mix-up they couldn't find any other relatives."

"What? Okay, I knew Allie wasn't his daughter, but he is still connected. This is getting more confusing by the minute. How about rechecking to see if anything new can be uncovered? I'd appreciate it."

"Will do, old Buddy. I'll email you his picture. Give me a couple of days to dig deeper. You got my interest now."

The picture didn't show anyone Hunter was familiar with, but he tacked it on the bottom of the typing paper and taped it to the wall behind his desk.

When he put the phone back on the hook, Hunter shook his head, but didn't clear it. It looked like Dallas' troubles somehow followed him to Cleveland. He couldn't shake the Texas dust off of his boots, so he'd have to see what was in that dust to put this jigsaw puzzle together. Somehow, though, he'd first have to acquire all of the pieces.

*   *   *

Motivation became the first of the keywords Hunter addressed. Who had something to gain by Allie's death? What was it?

When Hunter pulled out the birth certificates for Callie and Allie from the envelope found in Mrs. Lewis' desk, he knew Allie wasn't Billy's child; she belonged to the Fogg's. But it seemed the parents wanted to get rid of the imperfect child, so Ila took her.

Other thoughts floated around randomly in his head. Billy would need money for drugs. How could he get it? Blackmail came to mind. Who'd pay ransom? Hunter made two fists and beat them against each other. *I've been solving cases for a long time. Some were doozies. Why the Hell can't I figure this one out? Damn!*

"Hey, hey!" Zita stopped at his office door. "What's the problem? Your face is as fallen as a bombed building." She stared straight ahead. Her mouth fell open. Then she walked to the picture of Billy and jabbed it with her forefinger. "I remember him." She laughed loudly. "Last winter, just before you moved here, I was patrolling out by the Crossroads and I saw this guy running down the road. He couldn't move very fast with a guitar on one shoulder and a sack on the other. I picked him up and he was white as a pail of fresh milk. I asked him, 'What's wrong?'"

She took a breath. "You're not going to believe what he told me, Hunter. He said he'd been to the Crossroads thinking maybe the visit to the place old blues singers visited would bring him some good luck with his own singing career. Then he started shaking all over and crying out, 'Just the opposite happened. I saw an old woman appear from nowhere in a dress full of green tree leaves. Her gray hair was pulled back in a bun and she carried a stick for a crutch.' Then he stammered out something about her not saying a word but just pointing West, and he knew in his heart she meant for him to leave this territory. Of course, I could tell he'd been drinking, BUT the woman he described reminded me of Mama Cheche."

She chuckled. "He flashed a driver's license from Dallas. When I saw his name, I realized who he was–Ila Lewis' son." She grimaced. "He had shoulder length, greasy hair and cruddy looking clothes. I didn't bring him in. He hadn't done any harm. So, I let him out at the bus station. Since he was leaving, I took a chance and didn't make a report."

Hunter cocked his head and Zita admitted that broke the rules. "If you had," Hunter raised his voice, "maybe we could…" He threw up his hands. But when he saw Zita's face fall, he walked over and gripped her shoulder. "Never mind," he said, "I might have done the same thing. Okay, can you remember his first name?"

Zita shook her head. "It's Billy, and his last name is Lewis."

Hunter pointed to the door. "Let's go to the bus station and see if he bought a ticket to Dallas."

As they arrived, Zita turned to Hunter and her eyes lit up. "Wait a minute. I remember something Billy said when he got out of the car. 'You don't have to worry about seeing me again, Deputy. I won't be back this way. My visit to my mama paid off big time.' He patted his guitar. 'I may not make it as a blues singer, but I'll make it, er, another way.' Then he hoisted his guitar on his shoulder and grinned. 'You haven't got the foggiest idea of what I'm talking about, do you?' I couldn't see what was funny, but he added, 'Not the foggiest!' and laughed all the way to the ticket counter."

Hunter had an inkling that those words meant something, but he couldn't pinpoint anything. The clerk had a record of a cash sale ticket to Dallas that fit the time schedule and a couple of others bought on credit cards. With no more to go on, they returned to the station and Hunter added both bits of information to his chart. By the word "foggy" he wrote: *Motivation connection*? But the question had no answer.

After a long day of frustration, Hunter went home, fed King, and fixed himself a ham sandwich on rye bread, and washed it down with a beer. At 9:30 p.m., he had just turned down his bed when his phone rang.

"Hunter," Shannon blurted out, "I'm hearing noises. I think I have a prowler. Please, come over here quickly." She hung up before he could offer to send a deputy.

In a few minutes, he was at the Tollar plantation aiming his flashlight on the porch and behind bushes. Nothing appeared, so he knocked on the door.

Opening the door with a glass in her hand, she motioned Hunter to enter. "I'm sorry," she said, "but this murder of a child has me spooked. Maybe I'm hearing things, but I'm afraid that killer came back." She left and retrieved a glass from the kitchen. "Here, try this."

Hunter took a whiff and returned the drink to her. "I can't; I'm on duty. Look…"

"You're not in uniform," Shannon said.

"Doesn't matter, I'm still working." He faced her. "So, tell me what you heard."

She shrugged. "It sounded like footsteps on the porch, but nobody knocked at the door."

"Where are the kids?"

"They're okay, probably asleep by now." She sat on a loveseat and said, "Have a seat."

Hunter didn't like the close quarters, but he wanted to calm Shannon down before he left. He didn't want to get home and have her summon him again.

"Shannon placed her hand on his knee. "I'm usually stoic, Hunter." She leaned very close to his face, noses almost touching. "But tonight, I'm not comfortable being alone in this big old house that some people say is haunted."

Hunter's own discomfort intensified. This flirtation was going too far for him. He stood and reached for his phone. It didn't beep, but he pretended to receive a text. "Sorry," he said, "I've got to go. An emergency on the highway."

"Oh, no," Shannon whined as she emptied her glass and reached for the drink she'd offered Hunter. "Come again soon, Honey. And it doesn't have to be on business."

On the way home, Hunter forwarded all of his calls to Chan and turned off his phone. He needed peace, quiet and rest, and that was the only way to get any.

# Chapter 14

Harley's restless nights continued. He slept from eleven p.m. until midnight when a hypnic jerk awakened him. Startled, he found himself shaking. He realized why when a nightmare replayed itself in his subconsciousness. He was in his pajamas chasing after a criminal, firing shots at him to make him stop. When they reached Mama Cheche's house she stood out front, dressed in red, and tripped the person with her willow wood stick. It knocked the person out. When Mama turned to look at Hunter, she had no face, only a blank white area surrounded by gray hair. Then a mouth appeared forming the words *Fog and Motivation.* It ended there.

Hunter got out of bed, King trailing after him, and went to the kitchen for a glass of water. *Am I going nuts, or what? Why would I have such a crazy dream about Mama Cheche? What the Hell has this got to do with fog, or motivation?* He took the last sip of water from his glass and then spit it out. *Wait a minute. This might be a clue. Fog? Could that refer to the Foggs, and that crazy gal Rapier? Was Billy making a pun when he said Zita didn't have the 'foggiest' notion of what he was talking about? Motivation? Could the Foggs and Billy be connected?*

Hunter went out on his balcony and stared at the stars, hoping for inspiration from on high. A bit came. He recalled that Callie had no birth certificate on record and that her drowning was suspicious. He also remembered that Bruno Fogg had a fixer. Maybe he had more than one person ready and willing to do his bidding. Big money is tempting, even when it involves murder. It made him wonder if everyone really did have a price. But he hoped it wasn't true.

*Bruno, Rapier, Billy, Callie's suspicious death, Ila Lewis and the strange story of her having Allie. Hmm–Callie and Allie–rhyme. Never thought of that till now. What about the manicure scissors? Did Rapier have some when she was arrested?* He pursed his lips, turned on his heel, and went back inside. But not to bed. He opened his laptop and glanced through the emails Roy and Chan sent him, trying to connect the dots.

When the alarm clock rang at six a.m., Hunter put his laptop to the side. Then he sent a text to the office saying he wouldn't be in until ten a.m. He rolled over with a smile on his face and went back to sleep until the alarm sounded again at nine o'clock. Anticipating a shower, a bagel topped with cream cheese, and coffee with chicory, he hopped out of bed prepared to fill King's bowl first to avoid being pestered with "Meows" while he ate.

When King didn't come running, he called out his name. No response, as usual. Hunter looked around–under the bed, behind the draperies, even under the sink in the cabinet with the door cracked open. "I haven't got time for this, you damn cat! Come out wherever you are." Still no answer. When Hunter had exhausted all possibilities of hiding places, he slapped his fist against his forehead. *The cat door to the warehouse! I wonder if King is with V.*

He checked the warehouse, but still no cat. Hunter slipped on a shirt and some pants and headed down the inside stairs to V's studio on the first floor. The unkempt owner of the shop put down some metal he was working with and motioned Hunter to come over to where he stood.

But when Hunter came closer, he saw an unusual sight. On top of an old wooden mantlepiece, King strutted back and forth, swishing his tail but missing every knick-knack in his path.

"Oh, God! King was here with you. I was looking for him. I'm sorry if he's been bothering you." Hunter walked toward the mantle, but V blocked his way.

"No bother at all." said V. Hunter glanced around. "Interesting sculptures and paintings you have here. And I'd like to compliment you on the guitar you made for Goldie's gravesite. You do magnificent work with, er, with, I guess whatever you have on hand."

V's face beamed. "That's my trademark. Been at this for a long time." He stroked his beard.

"Well, I have to get to work. Let me take King out of your way."

"Oh, no, King's not in my way. He's my model. Visits every chance he gets. Striking looking animal. He got my attention and the sculpture I'm working on is him. If you have no objection, I plan to put it in my front window, or maybe outside by the door."

Pointing his index finger at King, Hunter said, "What? King's a model?" He laughed. "You better watch out, he's a scratcher and a biter. And a cat's bite is more dangerous than a dog's."

V walked over to King and took him into his arms, pressing his face against the cat's. "Oh, we're good friends. He's never scratched me."

*Damn! What's this guy got that I haven't?* He reached for King who aimed to scratch his owner but missed. The cat jumped from V's arms and scooted into the open elevator.

Hunter hurried behind him. "Thanks, V. I'd better get King upstairs and feed him before I leave for work. I'll see you again soon." He got into the elevator and took it upstairs.

To lure King out of the elevator, Hunter filled his bowl. It was 9:45 a.m. No time for food or a shower. Hunter slipped into his uniform and headed for his office.

When he arrived, he first told Zita the whole story adding, "V's different all right, but I like him. He has a certain *Je ne sais quoi.*"

Zita grinned. "Hey, Boss, if you're showing off, it won't work. I had two years of French in high school and I remember what that means. Yeah, V has it all right."

"Okay, so you win some and you lose some. Enough time spent on distractions. Back to work." He took Zita into his confidence. "I've been chewing on the Dallas Devil case ever since it followed me here. Let me run a few things by you." He slapped both hands on his hips. "First off, does it strike you as a coincidence that Rapier's sister Callie's name rhymes with Ila's granddaughter, Allie?"

Zita sucked in her bottom lip. Twins are often given rhyming names." She raised her brows. "Do you suppose two children were born to the Foggs?"

"The thought crossed my mind, but Ila was a midwife required by law to keep records. Would she jeopardize her career by not reporting accurately?"

"She quit being a midwife when she left Dallas, and she didn't tell anyone where she was going."

"Seems like Billy knew. I heard he suggested that she come here."

Zita tapped her toe. "And Callie drowned."

"You're forgetting that we cleared Rapier. No need to go there. It's done. However, who's to say Bruno Fogg didn't want Allie. He's the type to get rid of a defective child without having any guilt about it–just collateral damage." Hunter folded and unfolded his hands. "That theory shows motivation, method–murder for hire, and opportunity, the money to pay for the job." He sighed. "Problem is we have no proof. The victims are dead–Callie, Allie, and Ila. They can't tell us who killed them."

"But maybe their records can clue us in, Hunter. Let's put our heads together and see what we can come up with."

"Right, we can start with the sequence of events."

As he spoke, Hunter made a list of the crimes attributed to the Dallas Devil in order. "The first death we know about was Callie Fogg's about six years ago. I remember it well. It was very suspicious. We got the 911 call and went to the scene. The mother was frantic, but the father, Bruno, looked more angry than anything else. He was cursing and ranting and raving, complaining that the paramedics should have gotten there in time to save Callie. There was no record that the paramedics were even called."

He shook his head. "They couldn't have helped anyway. She was probably dead when they pulled her out of the pool. A neighbor called and we went out there. Odd, I didn't think anything of it at the time, but it looked like her hair had been cut but it was a tangled mess, and we couldn't be sure. Another thing that seems more significant in retrospect. The mother and Rapier both swore they saw a man with a hood running away. Rapier said that man drowned Callie and he tried to drown her, too. Rapier was coughing up water. Sounded like her lungs were full of it. But they wouldn't let us call for help. Nevertheless, our investigation didn't turn up anything. It's still an unsolved case."

He took a breath. "The next one happened two months later. It involved a seven-year-old girl with cerebral palsy who tumbled down a flight of stairs at school. She died instantly. A couple of things tied the two cases together, a lock of her hair was missing, and the kid looked a lot like Callie. We couldn't take it too far. The child's single mother was insistent about a complete investigation at first. Then she got a hot-shot lawyer who sued the school, and she dropped the whole thing, and quit cooperating completely."

"Any reason to connect Rapier to that case?" Zita asked.

"Nope. We *did* check. Her mother swore she was at home sick that day. Anyhow, the kid was on crutches and very unsteady on her feet." He pulled on his chin. "A kid on crutches wouldn't take the stairs. We believed it was murder, but we couldn't prove anything. That's when we dubbed the person the Dallas Devil. Most of us still thought it was a man, not a woman. So, we stayed on the trail. He must have realized it because his next two victims survived. First, he took Janice, but he let her go. Then, he took Karla, and he released her, like he did Heather Harley who he thought was related to me."

"Makes you wonder, doesn't it? Two killed and three released."

"Sure does. Sadly, though, he returned to his murdering mode. Next case, Ila, though that may have been accidental. However, Allie's murder wasn't. It was vicious and tortuous. Deliberate, horrible attacks on that helpless child." Hunter's face turned beet red. "Talk about a hate crime." He stood. "No matter who this perpetrator is, I'm going to get him. I won't stop until I do."

"I'm with you all the way, Hunter. Whatever it takes, we'll bring that criminal down."

When the phone rang and all Hunter heard was a cackling guffaw, with no identification visible, he told Zita, "That's the Dallas Devil taunting us. Look, let's quit for tonight. It's time to close up shop." It didn't put a stop to their investigation, though. On the contrary, it reinforced their resolve.

It was 9 p.m. when Zita and Hunter left the office armed with information in better order and renewed resolve–ready to tackle whatever challenge the next day brought.

# Chapter 15

Over at the Tollar plantation, unrest ruled. Shannon had let the children stay up until nine p.m., mostly because she was edgy about being alone in the big house. Upset that she'd received no update on Allie's murder, she sipped her third glass of wine and paced in a circle. Angry that Hunter not only didn't call or drop by with updates, he hadn't even sent someone with any. He also turned her down when she wanted to get to know him better. Yes, she was tipsy…but it didn't cloud her thinking she may have acted out of line. She wasn't sure if he liked her the same way. He kept coming instead of sending out a deputy, so she thought…maybe. That was no excuse, though, for all she knew, the killer could be lurking in her yard right now.

Workmen had been around all day repairing windows and door locks. The house had more places that needed securing than she imagined. Even now, she did not feel safe. She kept hearing sounds. Reassuring herself that it was probably racoons or squirrels, she peeked out the front window and saw nothing but what was illuminated from the porch light. Lights activated by motion detection were newly installed and covered the cotton bin. If anyone walked up now, they would be blinded.

Going to the kitchen, she spotted something on the floor and picked it up, discovering it was the mojo stone. One of the kids must have taken it from her dresser drawer. She'd have to tell them not to bother any of her things. She slipped it in her pocket and poured a glass of Merlot. But she frowned on the first sip. Nothing like the pricey wine she was used to drinking. Not Dom Perignon. The night in D.C. with Mama Cheche came to mind and she smiled, letting her thoughts drift back to the night with Mama and Tippiny. Since Mama wasn't used to drinking, it went straight to her head. They had to help her out of the restaurant. Shannon wished now that hadn't happened. If she'd been sober, Mama might have revealed something about Goldie that nobody else knew. It was too late now.

Or was it? Without warning, Shannon's head was spinning. No way the wine was making her tipsy. She was used to drinking. Her thoughts drifted involuntarily. The title of Goldie's song, *My Light, My Star,* echoed in her brain, then flashed before her as if engraved on a piece of paper. The words *Light* and *Star* were underlined. It set her to thinking.

When she sat in a chair, the stone slipped from her pocket, falling with a bang on the coffee table, next to her wine. "I'm not going to touch you," Shannon said to the stone. "I don't believe in you, so you can't work your magic on me." After a huge gulp of wine, she pressed her fingers against her temples. "Good Lord, I'm talking to that stone. How crazy is that? I'm a sensible, logical attorney. Am I going nuts?" But the uneasy feeling that her subconscious had been invaded persisted.

Despite her resistance, the paper with the two words waved in her face. She blinked and a realization came to her. *Goldie's song Reelin' Feelin' had the clue to the murderer in it. The first three lines in a sequence spelled ELI, the killer's name. Maybe Star and Light mean something. Why else would I keep thinking about them?* She sucked in her breath and tackled *Light* first. *But what could those letters mean? L–look? I–into?* Nothing for the words' other letters came to mind.

She replenished her wine, retrieved her phone from her purse, and dialed Tippiny's cell phone number. On the fourth ring, she got voice mail and left a message: "It's Shannon. I have a brainstorm, but I need some help. I don't care how late it is when you get this message, call me."

While she waited on the return call wondering where Tippiny might be since she wasn't at her mother's old house, Shannon tried to decipher what the letters of *Star* might mean. The best she could do was to guess that the *s* might mean *song* and the *r* could mean *record*. Then she dozed off. But her sleep was still filled with erratic dreams about that same song title, with no resolutions.

A ringing of her phone jolted Shannon awake and she knocked it off the coffee table along with the mojo stone that was next to it. A chill caused her to pause, then she replied into the mouthpiece, "Tippiny, is that you?"

"Yes, it is. You sound like I awakened you. I had my phone turned off. Want me to call you back in the morning?"

Shannon straightened her back."No, oh no. Look, do you remember the title to *Reelin' Feelin'* skipped to clue us in to Eli's murdering Goldie? Well, I've got the feeling that the title of Goldie's song is a clue to something else–I don't know what yet. Anyhow, I've been having these weird feelings and I'm trying to figure it out. Maybe the first two letters of the word *Light* mean to Look into–but what? What could the last three letters mean?"

"Hmm, *ght*? Good, hard target? No, that doesn't make sense. How about *grand home*?

"Or maybe *great home, grandma's home*?"

"*Great home* might be it. Then what could the *t* stand for?"

Shannon sighed. "I don't know. *T* - total? Testing?"

"*Top.* I bet that's it. *Look into great home top.*"

"Hey, hey. You may be onto something, Tippiny. Top? It could mean an attic. Two heads are better than one." She paused. "But we still have to figure out what *Star* is an acronym for. Oh, it just hit me that the word *a* could simply be that the article *a. Song – a record.* All we need now is to know what the *t* represents."

Shannon's hand touched the mojo stone as she reached for her glass of wine again. "Oh! Tippiny. It's simple the *t* is for *to.* And it all makes sense. *Look into great house top* followed by *Song to a record.* Sounds like Goldie left that message for Eleanor, but she never realized it. Oh, gee, I've been going through things to use for the museum in Goldie's honor. Now, I can't wait to find out what's in the attic?"

Tippiny blurted out, "But we don't know what attic, so how…"

"No worry, Shannon. To me, great house means the one I'm in. The Tollar Plantation is the biggest one in this county. It has…"

A blood-curdling scream caused Shannon to drop the phone. Retrieving it, she inadvertently picked up the mojo stone and stuffed both in her pocket on her way to the source of the sound.

# Chapter 16

Shivering like a Parkinson's disease patient, Karla cried out, "He was trying to get in, but the lady in red chased him away." She pointed to the back door.

Milk mixed with blood made a pool on the floor. Shannon lifted the little girl into a kitchen chair and pulled a piece of glass from her bare foot.

"That hurts!" Karla jerked her foot back. From a roll of towel paper on the table, Shannon blotted the blood dry. "It's okay. I got the glass out. You'll be fine."

The ruckus caused Charles to come downstairs and rush to his little sister's side. "You okay, Karla?" He looked at her foot and his mouth hung open.

"She's fine," Shannon reassured him. "Don't step in that glass." She reached over and picked up large pieces of it. "Get some ointment, and bandages from the bathroom. And bring me a wet wash rag, too." He did as he was told.

Shannon hugged Karla close to her breast and patted her head. "Don't worry; you're safe. Now tell me exactly what happened, Sweetie."

Shannon reached for the phone in her pocket, but it wasn't there. All she pulled out was the mojo stone. It must have fallen out on her rush to the kitchen. "Wait here just a minute," she said. "I'll be right back." She needed to call Hunter, so she placed Karla in the chair beside her.

Before she reached the living room, the electricity went off and the house was pitch black. "Karla, stay put. Don't move. Charles, wherever you are, stay right there," she called out. Hearing loud cries from Karla, she added, "I'll get some light in a few minutes. Just don't move."

"Okay, Charles, where are you?" Shannon asked.

"I'm at the foot of the stairs."

"Then sit down right there on the bottom step. You hear me?" She knew he'd go looking for his sister unless she was firm with him. "Karla's okay. I'm looking for a flashlight."

His weak, "Okay," let her know he was scared.

As she felt her way from one spot to another seeking both her phone and a flashlight, she kept reassuring the children that everything would be all right. She may have convinced them, but she couldn't convince herself. *Good Lord, I lived in D. C. for years and I was never afraid. Nothing like this ever happened. Now, in this hick town where I'd expect to be completely safe...*her foot touched an object. She stooped and felt around. It was her phone. "Hooray, I've found my phone, kids." She'd never been so happy as when she turned on its light.

Her elation was short-lived however, when she couldn't get a dial tone. But she didn't relate that information to the kids. A howling noise from outside caused her to jerk. But that posed no human threat, so she regained her composure and headed back to the kitchen. No need to waste time looking for a flashlight; there may not be one in the house anyhow.

Reaching the stairs and finding a pale-faced Charles still there, she took his hand. "Come on, let's go get Karla and we'll all go into the living room and wait for the electricity to come back on."

"Why did it go off?" Charles asked.

*Why indeed? There had been no bad weather, no thunder or lightning.* "I'm not sure," she finally replied. Maybe someone hit a power pole on the highway." She didn't believe that. "I bet it'll be back on soon."

Leading the way into the front of the house, Shannon looked at her watch. It was at least an hour until daybreak. No other houses were in sight. So, she couldn't tell if electricity was only off at her house. Panic overtook her. *What am I going to do? Here I am with two young kids, no power, and no phone. I can't call the sheriff. A killer may be lurking outside. My pistol's upstairs. Should I leave the kids and go get it? Oh, Hell, I'm between a rock and a hard place.*

Her eyes lit up. *A rock?* She took the mojo stone from her pocket and rubbed it. But fear went from bad to worse as she heard more noise outside and then a banging on her front door. At first, she pulled the kids close and motioned them to keep silent. Then logic took over and she realized someone with evil intent probably wouldn't knock.

A voice boomed out, "It's Hunter. Shannon are you and the kids all right? Come let me in."

Relief overwhelmed her as she opened the door and fell into his arms. "Oh, am I glad to see you," she said.

The electricity flickered back on and Zita appeared. "I found the circuit breaker on the back porch. All of them had flipped. I turned them back on."

"I didn't see you drive in; I didn't even hear your cars." Shannon said after looking at the two cars parked out front.

"We cut the car's lights in case someone was hanging around," Hunter said. "Didn't see anybody, or anything, though."

"Why did the lights go off?" Charles chipped in.

Hunter shook his head. "Don't know, Son.

He turned to Shannon. "Did you pay the power bill? Ha, ha."

Charles and Karla stared at each other. They didn't get the joke, but it lightened the mood for Shannon. "I sure did. Three figures." Ignoring Zita, she looked at Hunter. "I'm sure glad to see you, but what brought you out here?"

"Tippiny. She called when you cut off the phone so quickly."

"Thank God she called you." She held up her phone. "I dropped it and when I found it, it wasn't working. I was in a terrible position. No phone, no electricity, two scared kids, someone prowling around and no way to get help."

Karla whimpered and Shannon realized she'd said too much in front of her and had stirred up the child's fear again. She reached over and put her arm around Karla. "We're all okay now, hon. So take your time and tell Sheriff Harley all about what you saw, or think you saw, tonight."

Shoulders squared, Chales piped up. "If Karla said she saw something, she did."

Hunter patted Charles' shoulder. "We know, Charles. I'm going to listen to her. Why don't you wait here, and I'll take Karla into the kitchen? You stay with Shannon and Zita. It won't take long. Bet you're hungry. Then you can get some breakfast."

"Watch out for glass back there. Better yet, let me clean it up first." Without protesting that as Karla's guardian she wanted to be in the room, Shannon beat him to the kitchen and got out a broom, dustpan, and mop. In a couple of minutes, she announced, "It's safe now. You can come in."

Back in the living room, Shannon turned to Zita and held out her hand. "May I borrow your phone? I need to call Tippiny and tell her we're all right."

Handing her a phone, Zita said, "Give me yours and I'll see if I can get it to work."

They swapped phones. While Shannon explained to Tippiny what had happened, Zita fiddled with Shannon's phone. When Shannon hung up and returned the phone to Zita, Zita handed her own phone back to her. "Ta, da! It's fixed." She grinned. "It really wasn't broken, just turned off and in the silent mode. I guess you got flustered in all the excitement."

Taking the phone, Shannon muttered, "Thanks," lifted her chin, and announced in a loud voice, "I may have been upset, but I'm an attorney. I don't get flustered."

In the awkward moment, Zita cringed. *What do I say to that? There's hardly a human alive who wouldn't come close to panicking in this type of situation. I'm a police officer and it gets to me sometimes. I just try not to let it show.*

For once, she wished Charles would say something. He did. "I'm hungry, Shannon," he said. "Can I go in the kitchen and get some cereal?" Waiting for the answer, Shannon took a deep breath, but before she had time to reply, Hunter came out of the kitchen holding Karla's hand.

"We're good," he said. "Karla told me what happened. Shannon, you can feed these hungry kids, now."

With his head, he motioned to Zita. "We'll take a look around outside again, and then go back to the office. It's daylight and you'll be okay."

"But Hunter," Shannon said, "I need to know…"

Hunter held up a palm. "Let me mull this over and then maybe I'll have something to tell you." He waved her off. "In the meantime, take care of the kids and get those workmen busy securing everything. Oh, think about home security. You may also want to get cameras and door reinforcers."

Hunter and Zita surveyed the premises. Despite his own advice, what they found did not reassure him that security, cameras, or door enforcers would keep Shannon's family safe. He put little faith in such mechanical devices and vowed to keep as close a watch as possible on the Tollar Plantation. A thought pervaded: *Even that might not work.*

# Chapter 17

Back at the office, Hunter made another chart. This time it included a map of the area around the Tollar Plantation. He studied how it was accessible, where a person could enter or escape, and what parts of the house had insecure areas. In other words, from what places the inhabitants of the home were most vulnerable.

He thought about the lady in red Karla mentioned. Was she real, or a figment of a child's imagination? Karla couldn't tell him if the "he" she mentioned was the same person who taped her mouth and took her away, leaving her in a swing in a neighbor's yard. She did say she thought it was. But he had on a hood that covered most of his face.

One thing was certain. Somebody turned off all of those circuit breakers. He got up, walked to the window and glanced outside. Stars lit up the sky; the weather didn't cause them to trip. *So, who was the intruder and why was he at the Tollar Plantation?* Hunter ran his hand through his hair. His knees felt weak. Exhaustion overcame him as he realized he hadn't had more than an hour's sleep. Zita had made a sensible choice and had gone home. He needed to do the same. He couldn't function without some rest. He flipped off the light, locked the door, and headed for his car to speed toward home. Morning would come soon, too soon.

*     *     *

Tense as a cat cornered by a dog, Shannon couldn't summon the energy to remove her clothes and put on her pajamas. She and the two children had stayed downstairs after Hunter left until they became sleepy enough to return to bed voluntarily. She followed them and fell across the bed on top of its cover. She slept intermittently until she was awakened by the phone in the bed beside her. Mumbling "Hello" into the mouthpiece, she only heard static as a reply.

Dropping the phone, she fumbled around to retrieve it and heard a familiar voice. "Shannon, this is Tippiny. I headed here to check on you right after you called, but I couldn't find my car keys. They'd gotten kicked behind the bed. Is everything okay this morning?"

Shannon caught her breath. "Sure, we're fine. But I know you're trying to finish cleaning out your mama's house. You don't have time to babysit us."

"I make time for things that are important to me. You're one of them. Besides, I don't have much more to do here. And I have some ideas about Star and Light. I think I know where to look for that record. It's not in the attic; it would've gotten warped there. The T doesn't mean Top. It's much simpler. It…" The static fluctuated and then Tippiny's phone went dead.

Shannon tried to call back, but she couldn't get through. She tossed the phone onto the bed. *Damn! Now I won't know what the T stands for until Tippiny gets here.* She looked at her watch. It was seven a.m. She had to put those thoughts aside. It was time to get the kids up and ready to catch the school bus. Slipping on a robe, she headed for their bedrooms.

At eight-forty-five, as Shannon pulled up the covers to make up her bed, the phone jingled again. "Hi, coming, ready or not. I'm on my way to your house, and I'll be there shortly. Get out the coffee pot."

It clicked off. Again, Shannon tried to call back but Tippiny didn't answer. She went downstairs, emptied the dregs from the percolator and sat waiting at her kitchen table, sipping on the stale coffee.

She didn't have to wait long. Ten minutes of musing in her exhausted state passed fast. The doorbell rang. Shannon hurried to answer it, but not without peeking out of a window to be sure it was her expected guest. It was. She flung open the door and held out her arms. The two women hugged for a moment.

Then Tippiny backed off. "Let me look at you. Well, you sure look okay, not like you've been through an ordeal. You're perky as a well-fed kitten. Good." She walked inside and glanced around. "I don't see anything amiss."

"No, the intruder didn't get inside." Shannon bit her bottom lip. "Look, let's go to the kitchen. I made fresh coffee. I'll tell you all about what happened. You're perceptive and objective. Maybe you can throw some light on this." In an unsteady gait, Shannon walked to the back of the house and Tippiny followed.

After relating every detail of the events of the night before, Shannon sighed. "You know, Karla could've imagined some of this, like the lady in red. She's heard things at school, I'm sure. Kids like to scare newcomers. And finding another child's body half-buried in our yard could've triggered…" She blinked back tears.

Tippiny went to her friend, putting her arm around Shannon's shoulders. "It's going to be okay. This is why I came. You need a friend–someone in the house with you." She sat back in her own chair. "It sounds real to me. Let me mull over it and see what comes to mind." She stood. "For now, let's get off of this subject. We need to do something different. I know what it is." She put her cup and saucer in the sink. "You know after we talked last night it suddenly hit me what the T in Star stands for—it's Turntable, not Top. Come on, I'll show you what I mean."

With a grin spread across her face, she led Shannon into the living room to the old phonograph stand with the turntable on top. Then she sat on the floor and pulled a stack of records from the open shelf below.

"Ha, ha," Shannon laughed. "If you think a new record by Goldie is there, you're mistaken. All of those are bought records. Look at the sleeves. They're all by famous artists. Nothing new." She held up the one on top with a famous artist's name. "See? Sorry, Tippiny, you're wasting your time."

"No, I'm not." Tippiny removed the sleeve from each one and checked the record. Until she came to the fifteenth, Shannon was proved right. Then she held up one record without a label on it. "Ah, ha. Let's play this one." She placed it on the turntable, wound the Victrola, and put the needle down. Looking at Shannon with eyes sparkling, she asked, "Are you ready for this?

A voice announced: *This one's for Cheche. It's called, I'm Only Human* and then blasted out:

> *I got the blues*
>
> *Oh yeah it's real bad news*
>
> *I miss my woman*
>
> *This life is sad*
>
> *Gives me the blues real bad*
>
> *I'm only human*

*I'm only human*

*We had to part*
*It really breaks my heart*
*That you're not next to me*
*I miss my woman*
*I'm only human*
*But our love's meant to be*

*Why care at all?*
*Knowing I'll take a fall*
*Are you missing your man?*
*I miss my woman*
*I'm only human*
*Will I see you again?*

*Life will soon end*
*This world is not my friend*
*I miss my woman*
*Won't be here long*
*And so I sing this song*
*I'm only human*
*I'm only human.*

The silent stares of both women said more than words. Shannon spoke first. With her hands cupping her cheeks she announced, "I'm flabbergasted. I've never felt like this before. I can't express how I feel. Goldie's voice transports me to the past. It's crazy but I can feel a connection to him, to the era, to the blues. I know who he was now." She reached into her pocket, pulled out the mojo stone, and held it out in her open palm. "Oh, Tippiny, you were Mama Cheche's daughter. Tell me, what does all this mean?"

Tippiny shook her head. "You descended from Goldie, Shannon. You may not like it, but if he had the mojo, he may have passed it on to you." She held up a palm facing her friend. "Before you protest that Goldie didn't believe in it, that doesn't matter. From the old wives' tales, even if he didn't accept the gift of the mojo, he could still pass it on."

She held up the sleeve from the record and a slip of paper dropped to the floor. Picking it up, she unfolded it and read aloud: *Mr. Lomax cut this record when he was in Cleveland. He did side recordings for musicians like me who didn't have the money to cut our own to give to promoters like Mr. Tunstall. I was proud that he felt I had the potential to be a star. But it's never been released. The problem was that I never got the chance to get it to Mr. Tunstall, so maybe you can do that somehow.*

Her jaw dropped. "Wow! Shannon, can you believe this? This is a previously unreleased recording of Goldie Parsons! We've found a gold mine. We need to decide how to protect it." Tippiny snapped her fingers. "I'd suggest we put the record, and the note, right back where they were and not tell a soul about them until we've made a plan. They've been there for sixty years without a soul discovering them, another few days or even weeks, probably won't change anything."

Tippiny smiled. "Gold mine is right. And Goldie gave it to my mama."

"You know what, Tippiny. Goldie may have meant to just *dedicate* it to your mama." Shannon raised her chin. "Even if he gave it to her, it's in *my* house, and possession is nine-tenths of the law." Her voice was firm. *Good God, this looked like a lifesaver. I'd saved enough money to retire but not with two children to raise. And it doesn't look like I'll have much of a law practice in Cleveland. For a moment, I thought my great-grandfather had come to my rescue. Now Tippiny is trying to shoot holes in that possibility. Also, she has Goldie's guitar, and I would like it for the museum. I can't jeopardize the relationship.*

"None of that is important." Tippiny broke the silence. "We can talk about it later. For now, what do you want to do with it? Just tell me." Her hoarse voice was shaky.

Shannon cringed. She didn't like this kind of conflict. It wasn't conducive to a good relationship. Shannon ended the conflict by suggesting, "Let's play it again while I decide."

The mellow words and catchy blues tune echoed through the air. Shannon and Tippiny sat entranced during the three minutes of the record's duration. After sixty years in a watery grave, a blues' man was reincarnated.

When the last note was sung, Shannon slumped in her chair. "I feel as if all the blood has been drained out of me." She looked down to see that she was clutching the mojo stone. She opened her hand. "How'd I get this?"

"You never put it down," Tippiny replied. Then she changed the subject. "Have you decided what to do about the record?"

"Let's put it back where it was for today. I can get a safety deposit at the bank tomorrow and leave it there. Nobody has to know." She wrinkled her nose. "Maybe I should tell Hunter. He's honest and he'll keep it a secret."

"Okay, get me a key to the box, too. Why tell Hunter? It's safer if just the two of us know about such a treasure." Shannon shrugged. "But it's up to you."

Before Shannon had time to ponder over that decision, Charles and Karla burst into the kitchen. They rushed into the living room with Charles asking, "Whose car is that?" Then he saw Tippiny and took a step back.

"It's mine," she explained. "Hi, Charles and Karla." She looked at her watch.

"We got out of school early," Charles explained. "They had a teachers' meeting." He turned to go back to the kitchen. "I'm hungry."

"There are chips and cookies in the bread box," Shannon said. But neither child replied. "They'll find what they want," she laughed.

"Kids are good at that," Tippiny replied. "Oh, I've never had any, but I've been around friends' kids a lot, so I'm kind of in touch." She then held up the record and whispered. "Want me to put this back in the cabinet?"

"Please," Shannon replied. As soon as Tippiny put the record away, she stood hoping Tippiny would take the hint and follow her to the door. She was in no mood to hassle over this now. She'd go to the bank tomorrow and rent the box. It would be safer there. She blinked, peeved about Tippiny requesting a key. She didn't like Tippiny's objection to telling Hunter about the find, either. On that issue, her mind wasn't made up. When she did decide, the choice would be hers. Yet the nagging thought of putting their friendship at risk made her conscious that she must proceed with caution and restraint. Because both money and sentimentality were involved, that might not be easy.

# Chapter 18

With the discord between herself and her friend, Shannon decided to tell the only other person in Cleveland she trusted about the record. It had occurred to her that it had been hidden for over sixty years, if no one knew it existed except the two of them, what would keep Tippiny from denying its existence and hiding it away again? Soon, though, Hunter would know.

After she got the kids off to school the next morning, Shannon headed for the sheriff's office. On the short drive, disturbing thoughts flitted around in her brain. *If I do have a say about the record, what will I do with it? It should go in the museum, but I'll need money I could get from selling it to finance one.*

A horn honking behind her brought her back to reality as she moved forward on a green light. *Something else. If Tippiny hadn't bought that house for her mama, it would be mine now. I have to stay friends with her if I want to get it repaired and remodeled to a museum, too. I hope I can get some support from the city or from Cleveland's citizens.*

She parked the car and opened the sheriff's office door, not quite sure of how much she'd reveal to him. She could tell that he liked her, but he liked Tippiny, too. Besides, Hunter had flipped off any of her subtle advances. Would he think this was just another attempt to get his attention and maybe a little pity?

She squared her shoulders. *Pity is a form of contempt. That's not what I want.* Her independence returned as she marched to the front desk.

Zita glanced up from a stack of papers. "Morning, Shannon. How are you today? What can I do for you?"

Coldness in the deputy's voice made Shannon pause. She'd sensed a bit more than a respectful relationship between Zita and her boss. She vowed to pledge Hunter to secrecy. Caution became her byword. If word about finding a Goldie Parsons' record got out, truth and rumors would fly. Someone might beat her home to search for it before she could get it to the bank.

Zita stood. "If you want to see Hunter, he's not here. He's out on a call."

With a blink and saying, "Okay," Shannon left. Outside, she took a deep breath. Maybe this was an omen that kept her from revealing her secret. She returned home, got the record, and headed for the bank. She was stymied when she was told that no safety deposit boxes were available. She clutched the bag close. The second bank had a box, but it was a small one. In a huff, she left to try another one. The third bank's largest size was ten inches by ten inches. The bank officer showed her one, but she didn't want to take out the record in front of him. So, he ushered her to a private room and left her there to see if it would work.

Discovering it didn't fit brought tears to Shannon's eyes. Sitting there with the treasure in her lap, she dried her cheeks. *What am I going to do? Do banks have vaults? Will I have to rent one of those and pay a hefty price? I've got to do something.*

She rose and the bag with the record almost slipped from her lap. Gasping, she caught it before it hit the floor.

When the bank officer told her they didn't have anything larger to rent and suggested a storage facility, she thanked him in a clipped tone and left. After phoning a couple, she found one with an in-the-wall drawer where the record would fit. But she was nagged by the thought that Tippiny should be consulted about this turn of events. So, she made the phone call as soon as she reached her car.

"No, we shouldn't put it in a storage unit, Shannon. Those places get robbed all the time. And they have master keys for the units. It's too risky. I think it's safer to leave it where it was." She sucked in her breath. "Hey, look, Shannon, I don't mean to be difficult. You helped me in my career. I didn't mean to sound possessive. I guess I'm just sentimental about all of this. And finding that record."

Shannon was tempted to tell Tippiny not to make excuses. But her training as an attorney taught her to act prudently in such cases and hold her tongue. Keeping this relationship intact was crucial. With a sigh, she replied, "It's all fine, Tippiny. We both got a little overwhelmed at such a find after more than half a century. You're thinking about your mama's connection to it and I'm thinking about my roots and my dream of a museum memorializing Goldie." She heard repressed sobs on the other end of the line and reassured her friend, "We'll work it out, one way or another, Girl."

"Okay, then you agree with keeping the record where it was?"

"I'll do that." Not wanting to lie, she didn't really answer the question. She hung up with a lighter heart at healing their friendship and drove back home. One thing she would do was put newspapers she'd used in moving around those records in the Victrola cabinet. After almost letting it slip to the floor, she wanted to protect it from other damage. She turned the key in the ignition and said aloud, "I guess what is supposed to happen usually does. Hmm, maybe it's best that I didn't tell Hunter about the record. Even a sheriff might be tempted…no, Hunter wouldn't, but he might let something slip and someone else could seek our treasure."

Halfway home feeling a bit ashamed, she chided herself. *I'm getting paranoid, and that's not like me at all. I'm one of the few who didn't become cynical in the metropolis of D. C. Now, though, a town of fifteen thousand seems to be able to influence me in a negative way. I've got to get a handle on my values. To be honest, it looks like the devil has me in his grip.* She made a fist with her left hand. *I can't let material things take over my life…* Distracted, she ran a red light and horns tooted at her. Still, she finished the sentence, *not even a Goldie Parsons' record.*

# Chapter 19

The investigation continued and police from all around came to the Tollar Plantation daily to check on the family. If they discovered new evidence, they didn't tell Shannon. But she discovered a few things on her own. When she left the cotton bin and walked to the front steps, she spotted a piece of paper sticking out of a corner. Stooping, she tugged on it and managed to pull it loose from a corner of the steps. It was a Snickers' wrapper, like the one they found before. Shannon went into the house, put it in a baggie, and called Hunter. He wasn't in, so she left a message.

When he didn't call back by nine-thirty, Shannon crawled into bed. No matter what was going on, Christmas was only a week away. Tomorrow, she planned to go shopping. She felt that all kids need a nice Christmas, especially Charles and Karla. One day next week, she'd take them to see Santa Claus. *I know Charles doesn't believe in Santa, but he'll pretend he does for Karla.*

Since it was Saturday and no workmen were coming, she slept in the next morning. When her phone rang at nine a.m., all of her plans changed.

"Shannon," Hunter said, "I need you to come to the office right away."

In a sleepy voice, she replied, "What is it?"

"Just come down. I'll tell you then."

"I'll have to bring the kids."

"That's okay." He hung up without a goodbye.

Sensing urgency, Shannon hopped out of bed, slipped on jeans and a T-shirt and hurried to the children's bedrooms to awaken them. She only had to go to one since she found Karla curled up on the foot of Charles' bed.

To her surprise, the kids didn't protest being rushed out of the house without breakfast. It made Shannon wonder if such a routine happened often when they were with Fredrica. But that slipped out of her mind as she ushered them into her car. Adrenaline pumped as she drove to the Sheriff's office eager to find out what this urgency was about. A million possibilities flashed through her brain: *Do they have a killer in custody–know who it is and are searching for the person–or just have new compelling evidence?*

Karla's whimpering and Charles' saying, "My sister's hungry and scared," brought her back to reality.

"I'm sorry, Karla. But the Sheriff called and it's important that we go see what he needs first." Without taking her eyes off of the road, she reached back

and patted the top of Karla's head. "We'll get you breakfast soon. Please don't cry." She pulled a packet of crackers from her purse and handed them to Charles. "Open these and share them with your sister." The gesture satisfied the children.

Parking in front, Shannon noticed the blinds were drawn on the windows of the sheriff's office. Thinking it was unusual made her wonder *What the heck is going on?* She made it to the door with the kids right behind her. When she opened it, what faced her was as far beyond her imagination as it could possibly be: Surrounded by a wreath of holly and some circling a mirror and with a decorated Christmas tree on one side, Santa Claus sat in a swivel chair calling out in a husky voice, "Ho, ho, ho!"

Charles whispered to Shannon, "That's the sheriff; I recognize his voice, but I won't tell Karla."

"Don't you dare!" She glared at the boy. "Now go up there, tell him what you want for Christmas, and pretend you believe." She gave him a shrug.

Charles stood by Santa and asked for a couple of video games and a soccer ball. After accepting a stocking of candy, he beckoned to Karla. "Your turn."

It surprised Shannon when Karla seemed uninhibited while asking Santa for a baby doll and a new dress. Then her mood changed when she stuck out her bottom lip. "Do you have something for the little girl they found killed in our yard? Shannon said her name was Allie." She cocked her head. "Can your reindeer drive you to heaven?"

Shannon didn't hear Hunter's answer. She had to leave the room so her sobbing wouldn't be heard. She returned as Karla walked away eating a piece of candy from the stocking Santa gave her. If she asked more questions like that, Shannon hoped some kind of logical answer would come to her. All she could think of was something her old uncle used to say: "Kids can ask questions adults can't answer." Karla proved that was true.

With Santa's visit taken care of, Shannon prepared for Christmas. It was an occasion Shannon hadn't really celebrated for years. This year, she took the children to buy a seven-foot fir tree which they decorated together with ornaments she'd found stashed in a closet. Even Charles joined in the merriment, as he climbed on a ladder to place the traditional angel on top, making sure it balanced vertically. She also planned to take the children to church, fix a turkey dinner, and invite Hunter to be her guest.

When she phoned to extend the invitation, Zita transferred her call to her boss. "Sheriff Harley," Hunter's voice boomed out.

"Hi, Hunter, this is Shannon. I was just wondering how the case is going?"

"Morning, Shannon. Not much new, I'm afraid. But we're working on it. How are things with you? I hope the kids enjoyed the Christmas party. They needed a break. This has been traumatic for them, I'm sure. They've been through a lot."

"They're okay. It's been a shock, but kids recover quickly. They're excited about Christmas, even serious Charles, even though he tries to hide it. He doesn't want to be disappointed again, I guess. Anyhow, I'm planning a big Christmas dinner, Tippiny's coming, and I wanted to invite you."

Silence, then a cough. "Er, well. You know I like to cook, so I bought a turkey and, er, invited Zita over. Chan's coming, too. Say," his voice brightened, "would you like to come and bring the kids?"

"Oh, I was hoping you could come here. The kids like you and they're used to you, like family. They need this type of connection–in their own home. It would mean so much." Pleading was in her voice.

"Oh, I'm sorry, but I can't renege on my promise. How about if you come over after dinner for dessert, would that work?"

Shannon's voice became solemn. "I guess it's better than nothing. Okay. I planned to take them to church and have dinner around noon. Would one-thirty fit your schedule?"

"Let's make it two, just to be safe. Got another call. Gotta go."

When he hung up the phone, Shannon slammed her receiver down. *Damn that Zita. She managed to get one step ahead of me.* A smirk crossed her face. *Well, I'll just invite Hunter over for supper–turkey sandwiches and cocktails. I'll show her.* Shannon vowed not to be outwitted, not even by a deputy at Hunter's side daily.

# Chapter 20

At the Methodist church on Christmas morning, Charles and Karla wriggled around so much during the sermon—one that was over their heads—that Shannon left before the services were finished. "Have you kids ever been inside a church before?" Her voice had a frown in it.

"No," Charles replied. "It's no fun. I don't want to go back."

"Maybe you need to know the real meaning of Christmas, young man. It's Jesus Christ's birthday. The day He came to save the world."

Charles chewed on his knuckles mumbling, "He oughta come back."

"What?"

"I hear the news. Looks like the world needs saving now."

"Don't be a smart aleck, Charles." She opened the car door. "Get in. Let's go see if you got sticks and stones in your stocking after that remark."

"I wanna open my presents. I've been good," Karla piped up.

"Yes, you have, Sweetie. I bet you got lots of fruit and candy." As Shannon drove home, she remained silent. She felt a little guilty for chiding Charles. He simply had never been taught any better. She'd fix things later.

But when they got home, the phone was ringing. She rushed to catch it. It was Hunter. "Sorry to bother you on Christmas," he almost shouted, "but we have a break in the case. I'm coming to your house now." He hung up without any further explanation.

Shannon knew Christmas wasn't going to go as planned. Still, she let the kids tear into their presents and dump goodies out of their stockings. It didn't take long. It was all done before Hunter arrived.

When Shannon opened the door to see Hunter's beaming smile, she knew he was really onto something. "I couldn't wait to tell you what we found." He held up a plastic bag. "Manicure scissors. These were used to cut locks of hair from victims. And we're checking fingerprints on them. If this turns out like I expect, we'll get that killer off the streets in short order."

While Shannon wondered why he was making it a point to tell her, he continued. "These were found some distance away from the child's grave. They were by your back steps. I think the killer dropped them, but first, I need to ask if they're yours.

Shannon shook her head. "I've never seen them before."

Karla came over to Shannon. "I found them and cut my nails with them. But I dropped them by the steps."

Hunter's face fell. "Oh, Hell! Little chance of finding any fingerprints on them now, except Karla's."

"Karla, do you realize what you've done?"

Hunter waved off Shannon. "Stop. You can't blame the child. How would she know? Forget it. Look, there's an off-chance we'll get lucky."

He turned to the kids. "It's Christmas! Have your fun."

Shannon sighed. "Okay, are we still on for tonight?"

"Sure. See you at six." He took her hand. "Don't worry. One way or another we'll solve this case. Who knows? I may come back with some positive results about the fingerprints." He left.

Despite Shannon's efforts to have the Christmas spirit, it all seemed fake. Even Tippiny noticed the absent sincerity. "What's wrong, Shannon?" she asked as they sat around the table eating turkey, stuffing and pole beans. "Are you mad with me about the record?"

She was, but she didn't admit it. "No," she lied, "I'm just thinking about Christmases past." She didn't share the information about fingerprints. "Save room for pecan pie. It's store bought, but it's top of the line."

When the kids were out of sight, Shannon showed Tippiny how she'd protected the record and they agreed to leave it where it was until they could make a decision about what to do with it. When Tippiny left at four p.m., Shannon washed the dishes and reset the table for supper. Then she took a nap.

When Hunter showed up on time, the kids were exhausted, and they went upstairs to play with their new toys and try on new clothes.

He didn't have any news. "We couldn't get results on Christmas," he said, "So, let's talk about something else."

Shannon was excited. He'd never acted so friendly before. What was going to happen? They had a glass of wine and turkey on croissants with potato chips on the side. However, as Shannon cleared the table, Hunter's phone rang.

Hunter grabbed his jacket. "Talk about a break in the case. I've got to go." Before Shannon could ask any questions, he dashed out the door in a flash, revved up his car, and was on his way.

Shannon slumped into a chair. *How did that happen before I even got him under the mistletoe?* No answer came.

The sheriff's mind whirled faster than blades on a windmill during a hurricane. First, he considered it a good thing that he was drawn away from Shannon's. She knew something and he went to see if he could sweet-talk her into revealing what it was. He thought back as to why he never married. He knew the life of a policeman's wife—one of constant worry. Every time the man left for work she'd wonder if he'd come home again. He'd also seen two brothers fall and had been the one to tell the wives they'd died in the line of duty. Hearing Taps played at their funerals was another traumatic scene. He vowed never to put a woman through such ordeals.

Hunter's thoughts fast-forwarded. What would be at the scene? Mrs. Lewis' abandoned Lumina? Fingerprints that might match some on the scissors, if any could be found? A rope used to strangle victims.

Second, this may be a big break in the case. If the driver was apprehended before he got too far away, they might have their serial killer. How far away could a person get on foot? Hopefully, Chan had gotten to the scene first and he'd be chasing the fleeing criminal. They'd get bloodhounds from Jackson, too, to join in the chase. He stepped on the gas pedal. *God help us if Carlton got there first.*

Upon seeing Chan's car, Zita surveying the abandoned vehicle, and no Carlton, Hunter was relieved. He hopped out of his car yelling, "Anyone hurt?"

"No, Sir. But we've got a car here that's never gonna roll again," Zita called back as she stepped away from the smoking engine. She walked toward her boss, rubbing her palms together. "Chan's looking for the driver who must have run away. Doesn't appear that anyone else was in the car." She handed Hunter a plastic bag. Inside was a torn white glove. "Found this by the driver's side on the pavement."

Hunter's eyes gleamed. "Aha! Bet we'll get some prints from inside this one." He studied it. "Looks like the gloves they use in hospitals."

A wrecker pulled up to load the car. Hunter waved at the driver. "Wait a minute. I want to double check the inside before you drag it away." Putting on plastic gloves, he climbed into the back seat and fumbled around. Scratching under the passenger's seat beside the driver's he pulled something loose. Holding it up he stared at a bag of bullets, those used in an automatic weapon. "My God!" he said aloud.

Zita asked, "What is it, Hunter?"

He got out of the car. "Bullets for an automatic. Did you find anything in the trunk?"

Panic gripped him. Was this criminal preparing to take things a step further? A massacre like Columbine came to mind. Was the thrill of murdering one young child not enough? Or am I just getting paranoid?

"We couldn't get it open," Zita replied. "I thought they'd have to do that in the impound."

Hunter rushed to his car and took out a flat head screwdriver. Ignoring Zita's protests that they'd already tried that, he made another effort to force open the trunk, but it didn't work. He scratched his head. "Okay, take it to the impound lot. I'll follow you there."

As they loaded the car onto the trailer, Hunter turned to Zita. "You didn't find a weapon inside the car, did you?"

She shook her head. "Nope. Sorry we missed those bullets."

"Okay, clear the area. There's nothing more we can do here. I'm heading for the impound lot." *What if this criminal had a gun, maybe loaded?*

Chan came panting in their direction. "I couldn't catch anybody, Boss. He had too much of a lead on me. I've called for the dogs from Parchman Prison. Maybe they can pick up the scent."

No sooner had Hunter started his car than his phone rang. "Hunter," Shannon said in a breathless voice, "did you just leave the scene of an abandoned car?"

Hunter's mouth fell open. "I did," he replied. *How can she possibly know about this?* She didn't give him time to ask any questions.

"Look," she said, "I may be going crazy, but I just saw what happened near the Crossroads. It's Mrs. Lewis' old car, isn't it? Go to her house. Rapier was driving that car. Get her quick before there's a tragedy." She hung up and wouldn't answer when he tried to call her back.

*     *     *

Shannon sank into the chair Hunter had been sitting in earlier. She felt drained of all energy. Her heart raced. Looking at the doorway to the kitchen, she shook all over. The opening was blank now but minutes ago images filled it. All she had done was picked up the stone and fondled it. Then things started. The Mojo ran rampant despite the fact that she didn't believe in it.

It all appeared as if on a movie screen, one that didn't exist. First, she saw a car racing down the road. Not just any car; it was Mrs. Lewis'. Then she saw the driver–somehow, she knew it was a female, another Mojo magic. Next, the car veered right and stalled. The driver tried to start it again, but the engine was smoking, and the effort was in vain. Then the driver hopped out and fled the scene.

Shannon's lips quivered. Was this a dream? I was wide awake, and I was standing up. When she pressed her hands against her cheeks, she realized the stone was still in her right hand. She stared at it. *Who's Rapier? How did I know her name? Oh, my God. It IS the mojo. And there's more. I saw a woman run away from the car with an assault weapon in her hands.*

Squinting, she tried to squeeze the memories from her mind. But they wouldn't disappear. A knock on her door caused her to jump up out of the chair. She went to answer it and wasn't surprised to see Hunter facing her. She flung herself into his arms crying out, "Oh, am I glad to see you. I need somebody real to lean on."

He let her hug him a minute then eased her away from her grasp. "What's wrong, Shannon? And how did you know about that car?"

Swallowing hard, she blurted out, "You're not going to believe me. I don't believe this myself." She opened her hand exposing the stone resting in its palm. "It's this, the mojo."

Hunter rubbed his forehead. "Today, I'll believe almost anything." He helped her to a chair and sat opposite her. "Now, take it easy and tell me what transpired." Folding his arms, he waited through a few seconds of silence until the words flowed from Shannon's mouth, words he could hardly believe any logical D. C. attorney, much less level-headed Shannon, would ever say.

After she finished and was shocked to discover Hunter confirmed all the details, she still denied belief in the mojo, but had no alternative explanation for knowing all about the incident. Nor could she come up with a way she knew Rapier's name. Hunter wracked his brain but couldn't recall ever mentioning anything about Rapier, or the Foggs, around Shannon. Zita wouldn't have told her, either. No opportunity for that. So, Hunter asked if she'd been out near the Crossroads today and she said she hadn't been out of the house. He was baffled, but he had to move on. If Rapier, or anyone else, had an assault weapon, his fears of a horrific event might result. *Whoever this is, there's a danger that killing just one child at a time may have lost its thrill. It could turn into a macabre massacre. It had happened before; it could happen again.*

Realizing stopping it may be within his power, he hopped out of the chair and headed for the door. "I've got to go see how to stop this." He turned to Shannon, "If you have any more, er, visions, call me right away. We want to prevent any other catastrophes." Hunter made a dash for his car; his next stop would be the impound lot. But even if they found a weapon in the trunk, that wouldn't be conclusive. She could've had more than one. "Dear God," he prayed, "I'm beyond confused. Please help me out on this one."

# Chapter 21

After dropping off the glove to be checked, Hunter reached the impound lot. An attendant opened the trunk for him. No weapon, but a brown bag with a Dollar store receipt for chips, Cokes, Snickers, and a pair of manicure scissors was crumpled up in it. *Oh, Hell, I bet she threw the Snickers' wrappers out the window but that's Rapier–kind of firms up who she is for me, but we'll need more physical proof to prove our case.* He slipped the bag and receipt into a larger one and then removed his plastic gloves. *Maybe we'll get some prints from that glove she dropped.*

His phone rang at that moment. Chan said, "We got some prints from the glove, Hunter. And I took the liberty of faxing them to Roy. Guess what? We're in luck. He got a match from way back. Both belong to Rapier Fogg."

"Hey, Chan, you did good. Finally, we know who we're looking for." With a heavy sigh, he added, "Now all we have to do is find her."

ALL was the key word. Hunter realized finding and arresting Rapier Fogg wasn't going to be easy. She was slick and evasive. She'd proved that she could fool people into helping her. She could probably hitch a ride back to Dallas to seek help. One thing was on Hunter's side: It wasn't likely that the Fixer would be involved; Rapier's father had little use for his daughter. On the other hand, her mother showed she still loved her errant, only living child. Would she be able to help?

Hunter pulled out a handkerchief and wiped his brow. What if Rapier didn't go back to Dallas? Maybe she'd stick around and try to harm a classroom of children, mimicking the Columbine tragedy just before the turn of the century. *Oh, damn! I can't let that happen. Wait a minute, school's still out for Christmas holidays. I've got a few days to get my act together.*

But the week passed without incident. The search for Rapier and the **Be On Lookout** for the criminal that went nationwide produced no results. Feeling certain that Rapier would make her target Charles' and Karla's school, he assigned guards beginning the second day of January, the day school resumed sessions. NewYear's Eve, when the clock struck midnight, Hunter heard the TV reporter announce it was the New Year. All he could think of was how unlucky the old one had been. That brought to mind the Mojo. No word from Shannon. So she must not have had any more visions. Could the Mojo bring good luck? He hoped so.

On New Year's Day, Hunter drove around town and he passed the school three times. Nothing was amiss. At six p.m., back in his loft, he fixed himself a BLT and washed it down with a beer. But he hardly tasted any of it. His mind was focused on what might happen the day school reopened. He racked his brain trying to convince himself he'd done everything possible to prevent chaos. In an uncommon gesture, he got down on his knees and prayed that nothing would happen tomorrow. He pleaded with God to keep the children of Cleveland safe from a monstrous act.

When nothing did happen the next day, Hunter was relieved, but he knew the danger wasn't over. A serial killer who may have progressed to a mass killer of children could still act at any time. She could be toying with him. So, Hunter didn't lower his guard.

While dozing at three a.m. Hunter heard the *Rawhide* jingle of his phone and snatched it up.

"It's me," Shannon said. "I had another vision. Oh, Hunter, this is too real. I can't deny what's happening. The other scene came true. Now, I just saw, oh, it was awful. The school was on fire. I called the fire department, and I left the kids home alone long enough to go check it out. They'd checked the entire building but they said they didn't see fire anywhere. Am I crazy, Hunter? Is this the Mojo predicting something?"

"Just calm down, Shannon. You did the right thing by calling the fire department. You must have had a nightmare. Look, forget the Mojo and try to go back to sleep. We all have bad dreams occasionally, probably triggered by events and we've had some doozies this past week.

"But, Hunter, this is so real and so scary."

"I know, but it will pass." He wished that would happen soon. "I promise you I'll go to the school at daybreak and check everything out. I'm sure your dream's just a false alarm." But he wasn't sure at all. He tossed and turned the rest of the night. At daybreak, he fulfilled his promise and went straight to the school. Finding nothing out of order, he went to Levenia's for breakfast, something he hadn't done recently.

"Well, well, look what the cat dragged in." Levenia came over to give Hunter a hug. "Long time, no see."

"My job's been keeping me busy." He pointed an index finger at her. "You must never sleep, Levenia. I've never been here when you were gone."

"Ha, I take my forty winks in the back sometimes. Okay, let me get your breakfast before we get real busy."

She came back with a plate of eggs, bacon, and pancakes. "Did I forget anything?" she asked as she placed the dish in front of him and replenished the coffee she'd served him minutes before.

"Nope, looks great." He dug into the pancakes and asked, "Any news for me? Have you heard that we know who the criminal is now?"

"I heard. That dopey Rapier Fogg. I don't know her. She hasn't been here. But from all accounts, she's the lowest form of vermin, preying on innocent kids. Uh, oh, I see a stranger." She left to seat the unknown customer.

Hunter glanced at the newcomer, an old woman with frizzy gray hair poking out from under a wide-brimmed hat. She'd walked in on shaky legs, almost tripping on her ankle length skirt, soiled with food stains. Large dark sunglasses hid her eyes. *Poor lady, wonder where she came from? Probably an elderly relative of a row house tenant. If a shooter came in here, she'd be a victim—no way she could run.*

He turned his attention to his food. When he took the last bite and reached for his wallet, he noticed the lone woman walking out of the diner. She seemed to have new zip in her step. Maybe the food rejuvenated her. As she exited the place, Hunter saw her go straight to a motorcycle parked out front. The biker looked up through the wind visor of the helmet straight at Harley, giving him a devilish grin that he'd recognize anywhere. She raced away before he could catch his breath. Dashing out the door without paying his bill, he turned on his phone and alerted his deputies to try to head her off. The trouble was she turned a corner and headed in the direction of the Interstate. With the ability to dart in and out of traffic, escape was likely.

Hunter's efforts to pursue Rapier were useless. She'd eluded him again. He checked and found out the bike had been stolen from a private residence. Worse yet, they found it ditched on a side road, with no sign of the rider. Hunter deduced that she probably hitched a ride and was long gone. Was this a good sign? Would she leave the area or double back to carry out a devious plan?

The woman had "nerve" personified. There was no predicting what she'd do?

Going back to the school just in case, Hunter again found all was quiet. A guard was at every exit. They had no disturbance to report. He didn't get two blocks away, though, before he had a call. "Sheriff come quick!? a guard screamed into the phone. "We got a fire! I called it in but it's blazing away."

"Where is it?" Hunter asked as he wheeled his car around.

"It's in the kitchen. Musta started there. Don't look like no outsider is involved, but I can't be sure."

"Don't leave your post. I'm on my way." *A fire. Just like Shannon said she saw. What the hell's going on here?*

He reached the school to find the deputy had left his post to help put out the fire. He rushed to the first classroom to find students being ushered out of the building following orders they'd learned in fire drills. The same was happening all down the hall. Spotting Karla, he made a circle with his index finger and thumb, signaling that all was okay. She faked a smile.

Then he saw Charles who shook his head upon seeing the same signal. He also ignored Hunter's thumbs up. Still, he marched out of the building without balking.

The firemen doused water on the kitchen table, chairs, and everywhere the fire had spread. Hunter asked one of them how the fire started, and they pointed to a broken window. Under it, he found a stick with a rag attached. Stooping to smell it, he could tell it was doused with gasoline. Probably an extra one that wasn't used to start the fire.

Hearing a scream, Hunter looked out of the window and was horrified at the sight he saw. It was the woman from the restaurant, aka Rapier Fogg, rolling in the grass in the woods behind the school to put out her skirt that was on fire. She'd fallen prey to her own evil act before she could complete her horrible deed. Hunter saw her rise and dash off on a bicycle parked by a tree. Once again, the chase was on.

After driving around a couple of blocks where Hunter knew the bike path came out on another street, he slowed down while he looked as far as he could see in both directions. No bicycle was in sight on the sidewalk. He pulled up and got out of his car thinking Rapier may not have made it here yet. He also looked down the path but saw no sign of her. Could she have turned around and gone back to the school? He hoped not but went back to check. One block away he spotted a bicycle close to the school. Not only was it Rapier but she had a passenger on the crossbar, Charles. When he came close, she pointed to the AK 47 in her lap. Still pedaling she screamed, "Don't follow me or I'll kill him."

Moving close to the curb at a snail's speed, he called back in a voice as calm as he could muster, "Okay, Rapier, just stop and let's talk."

"I'll get away, Sheriff," Charles said before she clamped one hand over his mouth.

Rapier slowed enough to press the weapon against Charles' head. She didn't have to say more, Hunter held up his hands and stopped the car. He knew she'd keep her word. She'd already committed murder; she had nothing to lose.

He watched her drive out of sight while using his phone to alert other officers. He told them to try to pick up the trail in unmarked cars, but to act with caution. Then he drove back to the school to check on the other kids, especially Karla.

By the time he arrived, Shannon was there to pick up Karla who sat on the school steps crying in her arms. "My brother. She got my brother." She looked at Hunter with soulful eyes. "Can you save him, Sheriff?"

He stooped to her level. "I'll sure try, Karla. My men and I are working on it." He took her hand. "We'll do it." He hoped his promise wasn't a hollow one.

Shannon stood and he saw a vacant look in her eyes. They seemed focused on something that didn't exist. "What's wrong, Shannon? Are you seeing something?"

She didn't look at him, but she smiled. "It's Charles; he's on his way back."

Hunter stared in the same direction Shannon was looking. "I don't see anybody." A minute later, he saw a young boy racing in their direction. "Hey, you're right. Here he comes. Do you have X-ray vision?"

Charles reached Shannon first panting out, "I bit her arm hard and then I jumped off of the bike. She called me a name, and when she stopped, she dropped the gun. Then she picked it up just as I looked back when I turned a corner." His eyes widened. "Then I guess she tore off in that direction." He pointed straight ahead. "I'm lucky she didn't chase me and shoot me." His knees were knocking.

Hunter helped him to the steps and sat him down. "You were, Son. And you were brave." He patted Charles' head. Maybe I'll deputize you when you're old enough." He texted Chan and Zita and gave them an update on Rapier's location. When he turned around, Shannon had an arm around each one of the children beside her. All were quiet. It was a solemn moment.

The elusive Rapier wasn't caught that day, but the next morning the deputies went out in force. More bloodhounds arrived from Jackson along with additional policemen and policewomen. Locals also joined the search party but were instructed to stay behind the front lines. Other states were alerted in case she escaped the Cleveland net. They had her name and a description. Using his photographic memory, Charles told them she didn't have on a wig and that she'd ditched the skirt for Jeans and a black T-shirt. And she was barefoot and that would hinder her progress some. They planned to retrieve the skirt and let the bloodhounds sniff it for a scent. That was a bonus they expected to bring success.

But things didn't turn out that simple. Charles had seen some shoestrings sticking out of a side pocket in her backpack. Hunter surmised that she'd used Mrs. Lewis' old lady shoes for her costume and planned to play that part to get into the school, maybe as a grandmother. Then she'd switch later to the spare. Since she didn't get to carry out her plan, that didn't happen. Another thing didn't pan out, the skirt. Before they found it, it had burned to a crisp. Only ashes were left.

Hunter was livid in his disappointment. *Strike two. One more and I'm out. How bad can my luck get?* He'd switched to his personal vehicle, changed into civilian clothes to avoid being recognized, and had been casing the city and beyond for hours with no sign of Rapier. *Where the hell can she have gotten off to?* He craned his neck in every direction. Nobody was in sight. It was late and he hadn't eaten all day. He was hungry. He drove to Levenia's Diner to pick up a hamburger.

What he saw by the door shocked him. He recognized the bike Rapier had stolen with its kickstand down parked right at the diner's front door. Hunter rushed inside and grabbed Levenia's arm. "Did you see her?"

She frowned. "See who?" She pulled loose from his grip.

"Rapier. The bike she stole at school is right out front."

"No. She didn't come in here." She bit her lip. "Wait a minute! I did see a girl dressed in black not long after lunch time. I was sitting by the window eating my own late lunch and I kind of watched them. She stood out front talking to a young guy who handed her a Snicker and an envelope. She must have been hungry because she unwrapped that candy bar, threw the paper on the sidewalk, and gobbled down the candy. Right away, they got in a car and he was driving. It was a tan SUV." She looked at him. "Before you ask, no, I didn't get a license number and I don't know the brand of the car. I'm not good at that."

Hunter got on his phone. While he waited for someone to answer, he fired questions at Levenia. The only one she answered was she swept up that wrapper when cleaning the sidewalk, but she tossed it in the trash, and it had just been picked up.

"That's all I know, Hunter," she said. Uncovering more details would be up to him. *Damn it all. That sneaky, conniving little twerp has slipped through our fingers again.* He started the car. *Worse yet, I'm at a loss as to where to look next.* An idea struck him. Maybe she'd left a clue at Mrs. Lewis' house. It couldn't hurt to go check, so he headed in that direction. As of now, it seemed that Rapier was the one who had all the good luck, but he hoped that would soon change. What could make that happen? For a brief moment, he thought it might take the Mojo.

# Chapter 22

At the Tollar Plantation, Shannon had finally gotten Charles and Karla to bed, but not until almost ten p.m. Charles had been humbled. He didn't say much, but Shannon could tell how frightened he'd been. Not a surprise when you're held captive by a psychopath. He also stuck to his sister like glue. He even insisted on sleeping in the bedroom with her in a sleeping bag on the floor. Not sure how to handle this, Shannon conceded.

All her life, she'd been self-confident. Her mother encouraged her, and she had a drive of her own. She'd made it through college magna cum laude and pushed on to great success as an attorney. Not many lawyers end up in D. C. advising congressmen and especially women, even today.

Yet now she was stymied. She'd never been a mother and she didn't have a mother to ask for advice. In fact, she didn't have anyone to consult with. It seemed ironic to be a counselor and not to know how to act as one. But this situation was one she'd never faced before. Until recently Shannon never had much association with children at all. *I'm not good at this role. To top it off, I'm dealing with completely abnormal situations. Who the hell has two children taken captive by a psychopath? That requires skills way beyond ordinary problems. How'd I get into this mess in the first place? Better yet, how do I get out of it?*

She didn't have an answer. Guilt flooded her mind. She felt sympathy, even empathy, for these young kids who'd had no leadership, no father, and no mother really present. How did they survive? But they did. And Charles' extraordinary love and protection of his sister astounded her. *I guess when you have no one else to cling to, a sibling becomes a surrogate parent. Charles is wise and mature for his age. Where did he inherit it from? Maybe some people are inherently good no matter what influences them.*

Hearing a noise, Shannon went to the window and pulled back the draperies. The porch light was on, but nobody was nearby. She checked the drive and didn't see any car. She felt sure Hunter assigned deputies to patrol the area. Maybe one of their cars passed by. Going to the back door, she surveyed that area. Nothing. Returning to the living room knowing sleep wouldn't come, she sank into a chair and pulled a throw over her tucking it under her chin. She knew it couldn't keep her safe, but it felt comfortable.

She closed her eyes and the world stopped. In a few minutes, Shannon was fast asleep. But her slumber didn't last long. Without warning, he eyes popped open. Lamps she'd left on were turned off. The room was aglow with no clue as to where the light came from. Muscles tight as a drum prevented her from rising. She stared down to see she held the mojo stone in one hand. *I'm awake. I know I am.* She blinked her eyelids to prove her eyes were open. *What can this be?*

She stared at the open doorway leading to the foyer. A girl dressed in black bearing a surreptitious grin appeared in the opening. She fit the description of the psychopath, Rapier Fogg. Beside her was a young man with his hands tied behind his back. His head hung low as if he'd been drugged. She stared at the AK

47 the girl held in her hands. *Or maybe he's dead.* But he moved his foot and Shannon knew he was alive. *Who is he?*

One more thing formed: a sign showing this was at the Crossroads. *If this is a warning, what does it mean?* Shannon inadvertently rubbed the stone. *Please, please tell me.* The stone slipped from her hand. The glowing light and the images faded into nonexistence. Lamps flickered back on. Shannon shook her head, but it didn't clear it. She had a weird feeling that she should check on the children. She took the stairs two at a time. When she reached Charles' bedroom and found him and Karla fast asleep, she eased the door halfway shut, went to her own bedroom and plopped across the bed without changing clothes. She felt as drained as if she'd lost all of the blood in her body. No need to call Hunter now. He probably wouldn't believe her story anyhow. He'd think it was a dream. With those thoughts came exhaustion. This time she went to sleep and didn't wake up until morning.

# Chapter 23

Hunter had driven by the Tollar Plantation on his final survey route for the day before heading home. Nothing was amiss. He'd set a patrol up to pass there every two hours even though most of his men were still chasing Rapier. He didn't want to take any chances with Shannon or the kids. They were vulnerable alone in that big house that still wasn't completely secure.

Taking the freight elevator to his loft, Hunter doubted that he'd get any sleep. He had too much on his mind. Much less that he'd been humiliated by losing Rapier. He couldn't believe she'd escaped again, but she had.

Upstairs, he took a cold beer from the refrigerator and munched on some chips. King sauntered in meowing and Hunter fed him. After eating some food and drinking some water, the cat rubbed against Hunter's leg. When Hunter edged him away with his foot and didn't stoop down to pet him, King sensed that something was wrong, and he paced in front of his master meowing.

Ignoring King, who finally settled down and crawled into a corner, Hunter sat in his lounge chair, but he didn't turn on the TV. He didn't want to hear any more distressing news. He'd been as diligent as possible but the criticism for his failure to catch the criminal stuck in his craw. If there was any news, any break in the case, or complications he'd get the report from his deputies. No need to rehash or belabor points already made.

He'd just drifted off to sleep when his phone jangled *Rawhide*. He checked to see an unknown number, dreading what he expected to come next. His fears came true. Rapier no longer tried to disguise her voice when she growled, "I'm mad as hell with you, Harley. You foiled my plans. I had it all laid out. I was going to be famous, immortalized. You had to ruin it, damn you! Now I've got one more reason to kill you. And I'm not leaving the area until that mission is accomplished."

"Where are you, Rapier? Just tell me and I'll come give you the chance."

"Look at the photo I just texted you and you'll know where I am. Come alone. By the way, I have a hostage. You'll see him in the picture. Poor slob underestimated me. Mama sent him and she paid him big bucks to bring me home. She threatened that my daddy's Fixer would get him if he didn't get me there safely. Enough of that."

Hunter checked his messages and saw the photo of a man with his hands tied behind his back standing by the Crossroads' sign. *So that's where she is. Damn, what a nerve she's got by sticking around here.* "Okay," he said. "I'll be there in twenty minutes." Stalling for time, he lied, "I have to dress."

"The hell you do. Come as you are. You aren't going to live to care. Here's the rules. You come alone. You can bring your pistol. I'll give you a fighting chance. Oh, in the off chance that you win, your prize will be the urn. I'll tell you where to find it."

*What chance is a pistol against an automatic weapon, if that's what she has?* He didn't vocalize his opinion. He'd have another gun in his boot.

"If I see anyone else, they're dead meat. So is my hostage, though I doubt that you care about him. I'll tell you the rest of the story before I execute you." She guffawed. "It won't do any harm. How's a dead man going to report my crimes?" Her voice deepened. "Fifteen minutes or I come out shooting."

*     *     *

Trying to act normal for the kids' sake, Shannon fixed a supper of spaghetti and meat sauce, along with a green salad, milk, and brownies she'd baked from a mix. Charles and Karla had a good appetite, but she picked at her food. She knew Charles wasn't really himself when he didn't complain that the brownies had no icing. That was further cinched when Charles gave her a suspicious glance but didn't ask any questions when she scraped most of her food into the trash. Karla was very quiet, too. When she hurried them off at 8 p.m. for a bath and bed, neither one protested.

She'd tried to reach Hunter all day, but he hadn't answered or returned her calls. Either he was busy solving the murder or he was dodging her because he didn't have anything new to report. The last time, an hour ago, the message was that his mailbox was full. She was itching to tell him about her vision, which he'd probably slough off as a dream, so she tried again. This time, she got a busy signal. *Something must be wrong with his phone.* She dialed Zita's number but clicked off before it rang. *I don't want to talk to her. This can wait. Maybe it was a dream.*

After the news reported nothing new on the case, Shannon switched off the TV and headed for the stairs. Recent events had caught up with her. She felt exhausted. Her only reprieve would be to get some sleep. She rechecked all the doors and windows, happy the door reinforcers were now in place. Some windows weren't completely secured, but they were nailed down. When she set the alarm, she wished the security cameras had been installed but all couldn't be done in a day. She felt fairly secure but decided to stay dressed. Rapier was still out there somewhere. If something happened during the night, she might need to get outside fast.

She checked on the kids one more time and then went to her room, leaving the door to the hall cracked open. Laying across the bed and folding her hands in prayer, she raised her eyes to the heavens. *Dear God, please let all of us, and Hunter, be safe from this maniac. Please let Hunter find Rapier before she harms anyone else. One more thing, please don't send me anymore Mojo. I've had enough.*

*    *    *

Less than a mile away, Hunter's phone rang again. Rapier snarled out, "You sent someone, you fool. I saw a police car pass. It didn't spot my van. Look, anymore of that and my hostage is dead. Plans change. You go to the Tollar Plantation. Keep your car lights off and head behind the cotton bin. We'll have it out there. Any false moves and I'll break in and get the kids, you hear me?"

"I hear you, Rapier, but let's talk. We can work this out so nobody else gets hurt."

"You bet we'll talk. Stay on the phone while you're driving. You're not going to call a deputy for backup. Keep saying okay every couple of minutes. Guess what? I'm going to tell you everything. So listen up."

Hunter drove at a slow pace. He was in no hurry to get to his destination or to risk anyone else's lives. He listened while she related her tale.

"First off, I was doing fine at home. Daddy never liked me, but Mama made him give me whatever I wanted. Then the damn twins came along. I lost more favor when Daddy fell in love with Callie. Allie was a different story. Neither Mama nor Daddy wanted a Downs' Syndrome kid, so they paid Mrs. Lewis to take her away. I heard Daddy say, "Get rid of it." Mrs. Lewis took the money, but she kept Allie, pretending she was Billy's kid. Ha, I knew Billy. He was my type. When we found out what happened, we got together and blackmailed the old lady. We threatened to tell all about Allie, and she didn't want to lose her."

She took a deep breath. "Things went sour when Mrs. Lewis got senile. She'd been mailing us money orders every week to a post office box. But the money stopped coming. Now you know why I strangled Allie. She hardly struggled at all. I guess she didn't know what was going on. Oh," the voice got louder, "guess what? I killed that damn kid at school, too. She kept tagging along behind me and I got tired of it, so I pushed her down the stairs." She gave a guffaw. "Daddy didn't like it but he had to get me out of that one."

"What about Callie, Rapier? What really happened to her?" Hunter asked.

"You know. I drowned her. Daddy jumped in to save her and he almost drowned me, too. And that wasn't any accident. He was livid at losing his favorite daughter."

"I see. And you kidnapped Karla, Heather Harley, and Janice Courtney, too. Didn't you? Then you let them go."

He didn't have to ask why; Rapier volunteered the reason. "Hell, yeah. I just wanted to tease you, torment you, make you wonder. I was leading up to the big one." A deep guttural sound followed. "And God damn you. You stopped me from getting my moment of glory. If you hadn't, I'd be down in history now."

He pictured her as a copycat killer wanting attention and fame. Did she realize she'd be dead, too? What kind of mind does this woman, and those kinds of people, have?

Her next words were, "I see you behind me; pull around behind the cotton bin. This is coming to an end."

Rapier got out of the car, shoving her hostage in front of her, with the AR-15 he'd seen in the photo in her right hand. The man's hands were behind him and he had a gag in his mouth secured by a piece of cloth tied at the back of his head. Hunter parked. Getting out of the driver's side, he slammed the door and leaned against it, leaving his empty hands in sight. Cautious not to make a wrong move that would trigger Rapier's action, he spoke in a low tone. "What's next, Rapier?"

He saw her hand tighten on the weapon, but she didn't raise it. Hunter felt sweat pouring from his forehead, but he didn't wipe it off. That would clue her in. Better to stand tall. He cocked his head. "What's your answer?"

She touched the tip of the automatic to her hostage's head. "Think he ought to go first? Why not? Naw, let's leave this wimp to get caught in the crossfire."

By now, she was standing up and down on her toes in a sort of rhythm. That action caused the gun to aim closer and closer to his direction with every tiptoe. Then she stopped dead still. "Okay, Mr. Sheriff, draw your gun. But don't make a fast move. I'll count to ten and we'll both fire." In a chant, she yelled, "It's time to die!"

Hunter blinked and when he reopened his eyes, terror filled his heart. He wanted to yell out a warning but that would mean immediate death to the person he warned. Before Rapier got past "One," Hunter saw Charles poke an object into her back and scream, "Get your hands up in the air!"

Instead of heeding the child's command, Rapier swirled her arm with the gun around barely missing Charles' head when he ducked. Both fell to the ground. Charles dropped the stick he'd poked into her back and the gun slid away from Rapier. Charles crawled forward to retrieve it but Rapier caught him by one leg.

Hunter rushed to the scene but not before Rapier had the gun barrel in a grip. The hostage saved the day when he kicked it out of her way before running off into the woods.

Rapier pulled Charles to his feet and used him as a guard. Her arm was clamped tightly around his neck with her elbow poking out under the boy's chin. He started coughing and gasping for breath. Hunter raised his hands high, but he held onto his gun. "Let him go," he said, "and I'll drop my weapon."

"Give me mine first," she replied in a shaky voice. "I can break his neck."

Lowering his hands, Hunter made steps toward the gun, but before he reached it Shannon appeared behind them, with a 38 revolver which she quickly pointed at the back of Rapier's head. Rapier also tried to floor her, but it didn't work. Hunter got in a couple of shots and one grazed Rapier's forehead. She fell to the ground unconscious.

A siren sounded. Seconds later Zita jumped out of the car, pistol in hand, calling out, "Is everyone all right?"

Shannon nodded, but didn't say a word.

"We're all okay, except Rapier. I shot her. Call a bus."

Six more patrol cars appeared on the scene. Hunter sent a couple of deputies chasing after the hostage. One came back in five minutes shaking his head. The hostage hadn't gotten far. When Rapier dropped her gun, it went off and struck the criminal as he ran away. They found him in the woods dead.

Hunter exclaimed, "Good riddance. That thug got a dose of his own medicine. He died without us even knowing his name."

The ambulance arrived and took the still unconscious Rapier to the hospital. Zita was assigned to accompany her. Hunter made a note that she was wearing a garnet ring on her middle finger, more proof of guilt. As they drove away, Hunter thought *With all the charges against her in two different states, she's sure to face the death penalty that both Mississippi and Texas have. She might be better off not making it now.*

Paramedics checked Charles and then Shannon took him back to the house. After issuing a few more orders, such as a call to the coroner, Hunter went to the house to check on Shannon and the children.

When Shannon let Hunter in, Charles sat on the sofa next to Karla staring at a TV reporter telling all about what was happening at their house. He looked pale and mesmerized without seeming to notice his sister's head leaned against his shoulder.

"You kids okay?" Hunter asked.

A pale-faced Charles nodded but Karla didn't budge. She just kept chewing on one of her knuckles.

Hunter turned to Shannon. "And how about you? This was a terrible ordeal. Could I make you some coffee or something?"

Shannon's bottom lip quivered. "I…I…I'm okay. I've already made coffee. Want some?"

"Sure." He followed her into the kitchen. "Look, those kids are shaken up. You may want to get them some help to get over this. It's quite a shock."

She swirled around and got close to his face. Fire showed in her eyes, but she kept her voice down. "You think I don't know that? I may not be a mother, but I'm not stupid. This is hard enough for me. But for children…" she broke into tears and leaned against Hunter's chest. "I don't know what to do, Hunter. I've faced crisis after crisis as an attorney and never lost my cool. But this is different."

With his arm around her, Hunter patted her shoulder. "It is bad, even for a tough old codger lawman like me. I think I've seen it all and then this proves me wrong." He held her at arm's length. "The good thing is their mother wasn't involved. But, trust me, it'll pass, and faster than you think."

"I just wish I knew the right thing to do for the kids. They're so vulnerable."

"Kids are more resilient than you think. Charles is super smart and even though he acts out, he has a lot of self control. He'll bounce right back."

"But what about Karla? I'm sure she doesn't understand all of this. I can't, and I'm an adult."

"Don't underestimate Charles' influence. He'll be the one to bring her out of it." Hunter sat down long enough to take a few sips of coffee Shannon gave him before rising. "I have to go, but I'll call you later." He kissed her on the cheek. "Hang in there; everything's going to be alright."

On his way out, he gave both Charles and Karla a dollar bill. "You were very brave today, Charles. But try to put everything that happened aside. It's over now. And take care of your sister." He patted Karla's head and left. *Can Charles ever forget what happened today? Could any of them?*

It was highly unlikely.

# Chapter 24

Sitting at his office desk, Hunter made out his report on the day's events. The fact that he didn't get the urn was in his craw. But he'd keep looking; maybe it would eventually show up. The case was complicated, but he didn't want to leave out any details. Rapier's mother would be sure nothing was spared to save her daughter. She'd make Bruno provide the best attorney in the area, or maybe the best anywhere, for Rapier's defense. Honesty wouldn't bother any of them. Lies would have no boundaries. There would be court theatrics, pleas of insanity, and anything else it took to win the case invoked. Circus day was coming. If a detail was missing or they found a technicality that would serve their purpose, it would come into play. So he prepared meticulously for any possibility.

He'd filled out two forms with many to go when the phone rang. Zita was on the other end of the line. "Sheriff, we've lost her," she announced breathlessly.

Hunter jumped from his chair. "She escaped again! How the hell did that happen?"

"No, that's not it. She did get away when we wheeled her into the hospital. And she ran down the hall screaming, 'Where are the damn kids? I'm going to get them and kill them all.' She snatched up a pair of scissors from a nurses station and yelled, 'Don't try to stop me or you'll be dead, too.'"

With a gasp, Zita continued. "The paramedics, a security guard, and I followed her, but we couldn't get too close. I guess it was fate that took care of the problem. All of a sudden, Rapier started stumbling and reaching for her head. Then she fell forward and the scissors went right through her chest. Oh, God, it was awful! A doctor standing by examined her and pronounced her dead on the scene."

"Poetic justice."

"What?"

"Nothing really." *This will save the state a trial. Hell, it'll save Texas a trial, too.*

Hunter called Roy; he was in for a surprise. "I was just going to call you. You'll never guess what happened. We don't know why, but Frederica Edwards came to Dallas and we've taken her into custody on drug charges. She told us all about knowing you and setting that fire. What a flake she is."

Hunter sighed. It was a relief to know Karla and Charles were free from their mother's clutches, at least for a while. Hunter then said, "And I have a shocker for you." He gave Roy an update about the day's events and the climax.

"Great! It'll save us a whole lot of legal headaches. It might sound callous, but it couldn't have ended better than with Rapier's death. I won't pretend to be sorry for her. I'm damn glad it's all over," Roy replied.

Hunter agreed. The case wasn't over, though. He'd still have to finish his report for the record, but he wouldn't have to wonder about the results. Justice had been served.

# Chapter 25

Celebration time. Hunter decided to repay all of his staff and any others involved with a late New Year's Party. Life would go on. Because the criminal died, they wouldn't have to endure endless months of trials with uncertain outcomes, or Rapier being declared insane and later released to kill again. Something even worse would have been endless appeals, not to mention that Rapier was a master of escape. One more thing to fear was Bruno Fogg's Fixer. Even though the man didn't care about his daughter, he'd care about being thwarted and he might send the Fixer to take care of his revenge.

With the way things ended, neither Hunter, nor anyone else involved, was at risk. He invited them all to his house for a kind of debriefing and as a way to achieve closure, if that was at all possible. To keep it simple, he fixed four kinds of pizza—pepperoni, sausage, and chicken, plus one with all three and mushrooms. All were topped with gobs of mozzarella and sharp cheddar cheese. He made the sauce from scratch. He had a side of a Greek salad with Feta cheese and Italian dressing, plus pretzels, potato chips and homemade French onion dip. Cocktails, beer, and wine of several varieties were also plentiful.

The guest list included everyone involved: Zita, Shannon, Tippiny, Levenia, Chan, Carlton, and V. This was an adult party, with a discussion about the case and a debriefing.

So Charles and Karla weren't invited. But King had free run of the house.

Zita arrived first, next came Shannon and Tippiny. Right away, Tippiny went over and whispered something in Shannon's ear and Shannon beamed.

Chan, Carlton, and Levenia came five minutes later. The last to come was V, from downstairs. It wasn't a sit-down dinner. Everyone was served a drink and they filled their plates and then moved chairs around to sit in a semicircle. King rubbed against most of their legs and then settled on top of Hunter's lounge chair where he sat. He scratched the cat's head evoking a *Meow,* followed by a purring sound.

Hunter took the lead to start the conversation. After explaining what happened to those who hadn't been on the scene when he confronted Rapier, he stood. "If you don't mind," he said, "I'd like to get everyone's take on what went down in this case of the infamous Rapier Fogg." He curled his lip. "How did it affect you and what did you learn from it?"

"I wasn't really in on it," Levenia piped up.

"I know. But you know about everything that goes on in this town. Why don't you start first? Don't leave out how it affected you, if it did."

"Oh, geez. How was I involved?' She tapped her toe. "I guess by seeing Rapier go off with that guy. Earlier on, maybe I should've caught her in the diner." She cocked her head. "If anything comes of it, it'll teach me to be more observant."

"Okay," Hunter responded as moderator. "How about you, V?"

V pulled on the collar of his open-necked shirt. "I didn't have much to do with it. Just an outsider looking in. I, too, should be more observant. When she took that urn, if I'd been on my toes, I could've tripped her. I was that close."

"All right, Carlton, you're next." He didn't know what to expert, but he hoped Carlton wouldn't make this a platform to brag and even claim he was the one who managed to bring the criminal to justice by twisting everything around.

Carlton stood and took a deep breath. "I learned a lot about my own limitations. That horrible scene of a little Downs' Syndrome girl made me think like I never have before. God, I'll never forget it." He swallowed hard.

*Now that came out of the blue. I guess I'm learning you never really know about how people are going to react.* When Carlton swayed a bit, Hunter helped him back to his chair.

"Chan, what do you have to say?'

"Only that cases like this are unpredictable. You never know how things will turnout. I did also learn a lot more about research and how it can be unreliable."

"Tippiny, I realize you've only been on the margins, but what's your take on all of this?

She sighed. "I see lots of sadness in the world but this was the most horrific thing I can imagine. I found something the other day that tells me what Mama Tippi would have to say about it. She had no formal education, but she was intelligent, perceptive, and analytical. She didn't have the Mojo, but she understood it. And the Bible was her guide." She pulled a yellowed piece of paper from her pocket. "Indulge me:"

*Dis is de evil sper't what de Bible tells about when hit say a person has got two sper't, a good one an' a evil one. De good sper't goes to a place of happiness an' rest, an' you doan' see hit no mo', but de evil sper't ain't got no place to go. Hit's dwellin' place done tore down when de body died, an' hit's jes' a wand'rin' and a waitin' for Gabr'el to blow his trumpet, de worl' gwinerter come to an en'.*

*Ain't nobody gwine bother me lesen it be a spirit, and dey don't come roun' cep'n on rainy nights, den all you got to do is say "Lawd have mercy! What you want here?" and dey go 'way and leave you 'lone.*

After a couple of *Wows!* Tippiny said, "I'm her namesake and I'm proud of it. We've come a long way." Heads nodded.

Zita didn't have to be called on. She popped up with, "Wish I'd known Mama Tippi. She could've taught me something. But I have learned one thing–we have the greatest sheriff in the world. And I hope he stays here forever."

"Come on, now," Hunter said when everyone clapped and cheered. "Any other sheriff would have done the same as I did, only better and quicker. Look how long it took. My take is that I should've solved this case much sooner. I don't want any credit. Just avoid giving me any blame. And don't forget Zita, Chan, and…" his voice cracked as he added, "Carlton. I couldn't have done it without them."

As if on cue, King jumped into his lap and everyone cheered again. "One more thing," Hunter added, "I've learned that city folks and country folks aren't really too different. There's good and evil everywhere. My team represents the good people in the world." His eyes focused on Zita who smiled. Her positive, optimistic attitude reminded him of his mother. Like Ruby, she was stoic, strong, and resourceful. She knew what to do when, and she did it.

Knowing it was her turn, Shannon stood. Hunter made a comparison to the two women. *They're both pretty and upbeat, but Shannon is too aggressive. Even though she's a high-class attorney, she can be dependent, even a clinger. She's not as sure of herself as she pretends to be. And she has those two kids.* He wrinkled his brow. *Why am I analyzing them? I don't intend to get involved with either one.*

But Shannon seemed completely self-confident when she boomed out "If you want to know how it all affected me, you're in for a long diatribe."

It got the host's attention. "O-kay!" Hunter said. "Let me refresh your drinks first." They all received refills, and then Hunter held out his arm. "The floor is all yours, Counselor."

Shannon took a courtroom stance, shoulders squared, eyes focused on her audience. "First of all, this made me respect the Mojo. Was I cursed, or blessed, with the Mojo?" She cast her gaze on Tippiny. "Looks like it should have gone to her. After all, she's Mama Cheche's descendant. Goldie had it and he didn't want it or use it. It was also forced on me.

She shrugged. "In reflection, I have to admit it did result in saving lives and solving the case. That is, if you believe in visions, or dreams. I didn't, but now I think I do."

"What comes next for me? I've adjusted to small town life and to being a parent. The children are getting closer to me. These experiences have caused Charles to calm down and Karla is becoming more outgoing and independent. She does a few things on her own now.

"Tippiny and I have become friends. She's returning to D. C., but I think she'll come back to Cleveland and partner in law with me. We've come to terms. She's letting me keep Goldie's record with the idea of my building a museum to showcase it and the guitar. It's where they both belong."

She folded her arms. "I've settled down, too. All I want is a quiet practice dealing with divorces, car wreck claims, and other less stressful cases. I'm done with constitutional law." She smiled. "Maybe in the mix will be a husband and a father for my children."

Shannon sighed. All was settled—except they hadn't found the urn. *Can the Mojo help? No, I won't use it, even if I can. I hope I'm done with the Mojo, or perhaps I should say I hope it's done with me. But only time will tell.*

Mary S. Palmer & Paula Lenor Webb

# About the Authors

**Mary S. Palmer** has a Master's Degree in English with a Concentration in Creative Writing from the University of South Alabama. She teaches English at Faulkner University in Mobile. She has published sixteen books, three plays, and numerous poems. *Boyington Oak: A Grave Injustice* was written as a play and has been produced at the Annual Boyington Oak Festival. A Mock Trial is scheduled as a second event. Her short stories have won the Hackney Award and the Eugene Walter Writer's Fest Award (third place). She is currently working on the second book of the Mississippi Mojo series co-authored with Paula Webb.

**Paula Lenor Webb** has a Master's Degree in Library Information Science from the University of Alabama. She is currently a tenured librarian at the University of South Alabama. She enjoys research and documenting her findings in *Mobile Under Siege: Surviving the Union Blockage* and in researching *Such a Woman: The Life of Octavia Walton LeVert*. Her latest book, *Mississippi Mojo…and Murder: A Tale of the Blues* was co-authored with Mary S. Palmer as is the upcoming second book of that series.